DENNIS AND GNASHER

Heebie Jeebie Holiday

By Daniel McGachey

Chapter One

Dennis was asleep. You could tell he was asleep from three simple facts. Firstly, because his eyes were closed tightly. Nextly, because he was snoring very loudly. And lastly (but not leastly), because he wasn't menacing anybody and the only times Dennis wasn't getting up to a spot of menacing were when he was sound asleep, though he was usually dreaming about menacing people at the time.

At this point, he was dreaming about menacing the Vikings. All of the Vikings! An entire nation full of angry Norse warriors! Not a fair contest, you might think; a full race of big, hairy fighters against a single Menace but he HAD warned them that they were in big trouble. And, when Dennis says "big trouble", what he actually means to say is: **"BIG TROUBLE!!!"**

So far, a thousand longboats had been reduced to a billion matchsticks by some nifty catapult action from Dennis. Obviously the catapult was a bit bigger than usual. It was actually three oak trees strapped together. And the ammo was a pile of rocks, each about the size of a fairly large bungalow.

How Dennis was able to carry these massive rocks was just one of those weird things that can happen in dreams, like when you dream that you're at school and suddenly realise you're only wearing your underwear or when you dream that the King of Bulgaria has opened a chip shop in your home town, or that your Auntie Gladys has taken to wearing wellingtons full of custard. Being a dream also helped explain how a thousand Viking longboats had managed to fit into the pond in Beanotown Park.

Dennis laughed with glee as fifty thousand Vikings, their long beards and furry tunics soaking wet and their horned helmets and swords going rapidly rusty, formed a line outside the park keeper's hut, waiting to complain.

"You're a terrible child, young Dennis," scolded a woman who squelched past in custard-filled wellies.

"Hello, Auntie Gladys," Dennis grinned. "So, it's this dream? At least I'm not dreaming about being at school in my underwear."

Then the school bell rang and Dennis awoke to find himself wearing only his underwear.

Then the alarm clock rang and Dennis woke up (for real, this time), tucked up in his bed. "Phew," he muttered. "What a weird dream."

Gnasher, who had just been dreaming about discovering a dog-food lake at the centre of a bone forest, nodded in agreement before trying to get back to sleep. He'd just been about to dive into the lake when the alarm had wakened him.

"This is no time for dreaming, mate," Dennis told his faithful Abyssinian Wire-haired Tripehound. "Remember what day it is? Mum and Dad are heading off on holiday today. We're going to have the house all to ourselves for a whole week... that's if the house is still standing after a week." (The last bit of the sentence actually came out as, "daff imf mwe owf ifs dill ftnadding fturr a whick," since Dennis's voice was muffled by the red and black jumper he was struggling to pull over his spiky haired head.)

"Gnee-hee-hee," sniggered Gnasher at the thought of the fun he and his owner could cram into a week without any parents around to put a damper on their antics. He bounded after Dennis, out of the bedroom and downstairs.

Dennis's mum and dad were already awake and were in the sitting room, blearily drinking coffee. They were bleary because they'd been awake all night, guarding their luggage from sneaky sabotage by their loving son. There was no way he was going to get past them and cunningly tip itching powder into their swimming trunks ("Just to make sure the holiday was up to scratch," had been Dennis's excuse) or replace their suntan lotion with GLOSSI-GRO Hair Restorer (Dad had thrown a hairy fit when Dennis pulled that swap before last year's holiday).

"Good morning, parents," Dennis shouted, making Mum spill her coffee. This made Dad wake up fully, since it was his lap she spilled it into. "All packed and ready, I see," Dennis added, ignoring his father's yelps of pain as he hopped off to fetch a dry pair of trousers. "You'll be wanting to get off quickly, I expect. Let me help you take your cases out to the car." Dennis raced to grab the bulging suitcases.

"Not so fast," Mum shrieked.

"Okay," said Dennis. "I'll go slower," and he sauntered across to grab the bulging suitcases.

"Er, I can manage," said Mum. She wasn't going to give Dennis the chance to exchange her best sun-hat for a magician's hat, like he'd done two years ago. As a result, she and Dad had been forced to share their hotel room with three hundred hungry rabbits (and they'd had to spend all their travellers' cheques on carrots).

Mum picked up a particularly bulgy suitcase. As she did, a voice came from inside the case. "Oi! Put me down!" Mum did as she was told. She didn't want to pick up a suitcase that didn't want to be picked up. That would be rude, she thought.

"I'm sorry, Mister Suitcase," she apologised, just as Dad walked in wearing a fresh pair of trousers.

"Why are you talking to our luggage?" Dad asked. "It can't be sunstroke, since we haven't even got off on our sunshine break yet."

Mum scowled. "Don't be so cheeky. I'm talking to it because it talked to me first," and Mum also thought it would be rude not to reply to her speaking luggage.

"Dennis!" Dad growled, suspecting one of his son's tricks.

"What's in the case?"

"Don't ask me," Dennis protested. "You packed it!"

"That's right," said the suitcase, before it burst open, revealing a little yellow and black bundle which looked fairly cross. "An' you packed me inside it, inna dark, wiv your rotten ol' socks an' stuff."

"Bea!" Dennis yelled, as his little sister leapt out of the burst case.

"Awright, big bruvver," Bea said, jumping up to give him a high-five (though she only had little legs so it was more of a medium-five than a high-five). "I was packin' alla me stuff when ol' clumsy zippered me up inta the suitcase. Good job I had a samwich, or I might have starvationed to deaf."

Dad looked at his once cleanly washed and neatly ironed and packed socks. They were now covered in jam and pickles and breadcrumbs from Bea's supper. But it served him right for not checking what he was packing, he supposed. Besides, he had another caseload of emergency socks packed and ready (as well as another, top-secret supply of emergency-emergency socks for really big disasters).

"All set?" Dennis asked. "Good! Off you go! See ya next week! Don't worry about Gnasher and me. We'll be fine on our own, here."

"Gnyep," Gnasher nodded, opening the front door so Dennis could usher his parents out with their luggage.

"On your own?" Dad was laughing.

"Here?" Mum was laughing too.

Dennis wasn't laughing. Something was up here, he realised. But what?

"Stand to attention there, young lad and young dog," a voice barked.

Dennis turned to Gnasher, who shrugged and gave him a look to say, "That wasn't my bark, boss."

"Stop slouching. Chin up, shoulders back, eyes front, arms to the side, mouth beneath the nose," the voice continued. This voice was coming from just below a very large military moustache, worn by a medium sized military man who stood

6

in the doorway. It was Dennis's next door neighbour, the Colonel. He saluted smartly to Mum and Dad, saying, "Colonel reporting for babysitting duty." He checked his watch. "0830 hours, on the dot," he said, awarding himself a medal for punctuality.

Dennis groaned. "Don't tell me you're going to keep popping round to check on me."

"Oh, no," the Colonel replied. "No time for that, young feller, me lad."

"Good," sighed Dennis, relieved.

"You'll be coming with me to Fort Fearsome Army Base," the Colonel explained, "where there'll be an entire platoon of specially trained babysitting commandos ready to keep an eye on you round the clock. That'll put a stop to your menace-type mischief, I'll be bound!" The Colonel chuckled. He then chortled. Then he did a cross between a giggle and a guffaw. "No-one escapes from Fort Fearsome!"

Dennis's holiday hadn't even started and already it was a disaster!

Chapter Two

Maybe Fort Fearsome sounds like the kind of place you'd expect to find loads of great, big, tough soldiers, all armed to the teeth, high fences topped with coils of barbed wire and fierce guard dogs on patrol. But it wasn't as bad as that. No!

It was much, much, much worse!

Fort Fearsome hadn't always been an army base. It was built in the Dark Ages, before the invention of the light bulb (and when the jokes in this story weren't quite as ancient as they are now). It was built by Lord Oliver the 'Orrible, the most unpopular earl in the land (except when he went swimming, when he was the most unpopular earl in the sea), who had so many enemies that he needed to build a castle secure enough that none of them could ever break in and give him a good stabbing. So he built the most invulnerable, unconquerable and invincible castle he could.

"Verily," he said, for those were the days when people said words like "verily", "forsooth" and "hey-nonny-nonny" (though few of them really knew what they meant). "Verily," said Lord Oliver, "'tis the most unbreakable-into fortress in these lands. Mine foes shalt never lay a sword upon me within this mighty castle. None shalt enter!" And he was right. It was impossible to break into. In fact, even he couldn't get inside. So he had to build another fort and, this time, he remembered to put a door in it, so he could get in. This second fort was named Fort Fearsome, since attempting to enter it was so dangerous (the first one was named Fort Useless, since attempting to enter it was a complete waste of time).

For a start, if you wanted to get to the fort, you first had to make it alive through the Frightful Forest, which was a forest full of frightful things (big surprise, eh?), like bears and wolves and very irritable squirrels.

Next, if you'd escaped being mauled, eaten or pelted with nuts, you would have to cross Lake Lethal, a very deep, very murky stretch of water which was full of specially imported crocodiles and piranha fish which, when they weren't trying to eat each other, would happily gulp down anyone trying to cross the lake.

Finally, to reach the great castle doors, you were going to have to climb to the perilous peak of Perilous Peak, the most jaggy, craggy mountain around. THEN you would get to the soldiers, the barbed wire and the fierce guard dogs... as well as the Phantom, the ghost of Lord Oliver, which was said to wander the castle, wailing horribly in torment.

And, if you think that sounds nearly impossible to get into, just imagine how difficult it would be to escape from.

Which is why Dennis decided to escape before the Colonel could even finish chuckling, chortling and gugglawing (which is a cross between giggling and guffawing), which he'd been doing since the end of the previous chapter. Which must come as a big disappointment to anyone who was looking forward to reading about the exploits of Dennis and Gnasher in a creepy, old, haunted castle. Sorry.

WHOOOOOOOOOOOOOOOOOOOOOOOOOOOOSHHHHHH!!!! (only quicker) and both Dennis and Gnasher were off (though neither had taken a bath in quite a while so it was difficult to tell which was the most "off"). In fact, Dennis hadn't moved so quickly since Mum had threatened to take him shopping for a school uniform and to the hairdresser to have his hair curled. Poor Mum could never have caught him, even if she'd been wearing rocket-powered slippers. And the last time Gnasher had put on a burst of speed like it was when he'd heard that a butcher's van had shed a load of bones just outside town. Though he hadn't been nearly so fast on his way back, since he was bloated with bones.

The Colonel's moustache stopped quivering with mirth and drooped with dismay. He was no longer chuckling, chortling or giffling (which is another word for guffawing and giggling at the same time). In fact, he was looking thoroughly miffed.

"Hmmph!" he spluttered. "Jolly bad show, escaping while a chap's gloating! Just not the done thing. It's dashed un-sportsmanlike, dashing off like that."

"Some babysitter you turned out to be," sighed Dad, lugging a very bulky case out to the car. "We're not even gone yet and you've already managed to lose our son and our dog! What were you planning next? Losing our house?"

"I have never lost a building, sir," the Colonel blustered. "Er... well, except for Military Headquarters after we tested out a new batch of camouflage paint on it. Bit too effective as camouflage, it turned out."

Dad, still struggling with the case, groaned. "I was being sarcastic. Now, will you stop standing about and find Dennis and Gnasher?"

"Oh, yes. Highly amusing," the Colonel grinned. "Terribly funny."

"What is?" Dad demanded.

"Finding Dennis and that dog of his," explained the Colonel. "You were being sarcastic again. I mean, imagine actually wanting those two menaces back." Then he saw the look of fury on Mum's and Dad's faces and realised it wasn't a joke. "I'll arrange a search party straight away!"

When word got round that Dennis and Gnasher were missing, the Colonel got his party. Not a search party, though. It was more a celebration thrown by everyone in town who had ever been menaced by the dreaded duo. Teachers, policemen, traffic wardens, park keepers and barbers, vets, butchers and softies danced through the streets.

Meanwhile, outside Dennis's house, Dad was pacing up and down and Mum was pacing down and up. Bea wasn't pacing. She was just waiting for Mum and Dad to collide in the centre of the lawn.

Just then, the Colonel came back into view. Shambles, his

faithful butler, chauffeur and cook was driving him along the road. Actually, his armoured car was being driven by Shambles, since the Colonel had failed his M.O.T. again.

"The whole town has been put on Red and Black Alert," the Colonel reported. "We've brought in special army sniffer dogs to track the lad down, using one of his socks to give them the scent. I'm sure they'll be hot on his trail... once they've regained consciousness, anyway. And I haven't seen so many people combing the area since that lorry spilled its load of GLOSSI-GRO hair restorer." The Colonel chuckled with military mirth at this little joke and awarded himself a medal for humour in the face of adversity.

"Well," groaned Dennis's dad, heaving the bulky suitcase he'd just finished packing into the back of the car back out again, "looks like the holiday's off, at least until Dennis is found."

"Nonsense," said the Colonel, grabbing the suitcase from Dad. "The little swine... Ho-ho.. I mean, the little chap will turn up soon enough. No need to spoil your hols, eh?" He was trying to put the case back into the back of Dad's car, though Dad was getting in the way a bit.

Seizing the handle, Dad tugged at his luggage. "We're not going anywhere till we know that Dennis and Gnasher are safe... and that everyone else is safe from Dennis and Gnasher. Now, give me my case!"

The Colonel struggled to keep his grip and throw the suitcase back into the car, protesting that, "I'm the senior officer here! You're going on your holiday and that's an order!"

"I'll go on holiday when those two menaces turn up," Dad shouted and the two men struggled with the case, which gave a loud RRRRRRRRRRRIIIIIIIPPPP!!! before flying apart into two halves, dropping a pile of Dad's neatly ironed vests and Y-fronts onto the ground.

"That's torn it," the Colonel said. "Shambles, pick those clothes up, at the double."

Muttering mutinously, the short, short-tempered butler bent over to retrieve the undergarments from where they'd fallen. Only they were no longer where they'd been. "Blimey, guvnor," he wheezed. "Them vests have done a runner. Look! They're

scarperin' now!" He was pointing at two heaps of undies that were racing for the garden gate.

"They've never done that before," said Dad, scratching his head at this unusual underwear occurrence.

"I can't have ironed them properly," Mum said, embarrassed.

"I'll clobber this clobber," growled Shambles, springing through the air, using the ancient Cockney martial art of Doo-Wot-Jonn! He landed in a heap. Luckily for him, it was one of the heaps of Dad's escaping vests and pants. The heap collapsed in a heap beneath him, letting out a groan.

"I thought as much," grinned the Colonel. "Dennis, you are under a vest and under arrest!"

Dennis poked his head out from the heap of underwear. "So much for my undie-cover escape," he groaned. The other pile of underclothes sniffed glumly around him before Gnasher's head emerged through the waistband of a pair of purple, paisley patterned pants. "Pant, pant," he wheezed (making another pair of pants).

"You've found them," Dad said, piling his clothes in the boot, bundling Mum into the passenger seat and strapping Bea into her SUPA-STRENGTH baby-chair. "We're off on holiday, then, before you can lose them again. Byee!" And, with a VRRROOOM and a final wave from Bea, the car sped off.

The Colonel was busy awarding himself another medal, this time for foiling Dennis's escape, while Shambles, armed with soap and flea-powder, marched both boy and dog into the back of the armoured car, in case they tried to get away again.

"Next stop, Fort Fearsome," the Colonel announced (which should please everyone who was disappointed earlier when they thought this wasn't going to be a story about a creepy, old haunted castle), " after we stop off to pick up more medals."

With the dangerous thoughts racing around a furious Dennis's mind, if the Colonel got through this week, he would deserve every medal going!

Chapter Three

Chugging along, the armoured car's journey was a noisy one. Not that the armoured car was making much noise but Dennis certainly was. He complained loudly, he complained at length and he complained using such naughty language that the Colonel had to stuff the ends of his massive moustache into his ears to stop himself blushing furiously (and you needn't think I'm going to print any of them here. This is a family book). Gnasher joined in by whining mournfully at the top of his voice and from the bottom of his heart.

"How dare you call me that," the Colonel roared, "before I've had a chance to look it up in a dictionary? You will rue that remark, sir!"

Dennis, who reckoned there had been enough rued remarks, glumly lapsed into silence. This wasn't his idea of a holiday at all. For a start, if he'd been in charge, he'd be the one driving the armoured car... straight through the walls of his school.

"It's hardly first class travel," he groaned, shifting uncomfortably in his seat, which was all knobbly and bumpy. He had to think of a way out of this but was having trouble thinking at all over all the complaining that was going on.

"Hang on a tick," he said. "I've stopped complaining."

He looked at Gnasher. The faithful pooch had given up whining and was now busily flicking his fleas at the Colonel's moustache. The Colonel, however, was keeping a stiff upper lip. He was trying hard not to shout, "Itchy-witchy-itchy-woo!" It wasn't the done thing for a man in his position to shout, "Itchy-witchy-itchy-woo!" even with a moustache bristling with fleas. In fact, he'd promised himself a medal if he didn't shout, "Itchy-witchy-itchy-woo!" (and, in case you're wondering, yes, I just like writing "Itchy-witchy-itchy-woo!" and it's MY book, so I can write "Itchy-witchy-itchy-woo!" as many times as I want!)

"Who's that complaining?" wondered Dennis, wriggling to make himself more comfy.

"Us," said a voice. "Will you stop wriggling? We can't get comfy!"

Dennis stood up and realised why the seat he'd been sitting in was so uncomfortable. Someone else was already sitting in it. Two someone elses, to be precise. Two someone elses that Dennis recognised straight away.

"Curly! Pie-Face!" he gasped, seeing his fellow menaces looking unhappily up at him. "What are you two doing here?"

"Trying not to get sat on," Curly replied.

"Wishing we were somewhere else," Pie-Face answered.

Both explained to Dennis how their parents had all gone off on holiday that morning and how the Colonel had volunteered to look after them.

"Funny, all our parents going on holiday at the same time, without us," Curly said. "Anyone'd think it was us they wanted a holiday from."

Dennis, Gnasher, Curly and Pie-Face looked thoughtful for a long moment. Then, "Nah!" they agreed, shaking their heads at the idea. It had to be a coincidence. Their parents weren't that devious. They weren't smart enough for that.

(Meanwhile, on board a luxury yacht which was just pulling out of dock, the parents of Dennis, Curly and Pie-Face clinked champagne glasses together and patted Dennis's Dad on the back for coming up with such a devious plan to ensure they had a nice, quiet holiday. As a matter of fact, they were celebrating so much that the only one to even hear the radio report of Hurricane Muriel, which was rapidly approaching Beanotown Bay, was Baby Bea, who immediately set out making a lifeboat out of ULTRA-WATERPROOF nappies. "It's all plain sailing from here on," Dad announced, wrongly as ever.)

Shambles peered out at the gloomy forest lying ahead of the little armoured car. An eerie mist trailed and coiled between stunted and gnarled trees, whose branches seemed to reach out like clawed hands. He didn't like the look of it one tiny little bit. He hadn't been made regimental mascot (after the goat was promoted to general) for nothing. He knew trouble when he saw it and, since he'd been working for the Colonel, he had seen plenty of it! There had been The Awful Adventure Of The Yodelling Clam, for a start, not to mention The Ghastly Affair Of The Trampolining Stoat (even though I've just mentioned it) and The Mysterious Mystery Of The Mamboing Mollusc and countless other escapades that are too terrifying (or too silly) to recall. After all that, nothing frightened him.

"What was that sound?" Shambles yelped, ducking under the driver's seat.

"Nothing," the Colonel replied, thus proving that nothing actually did frighten his right hand man (who was more like two left feet).

Just then, there actually was a sound. A long, shrill scream that could reduce the bravest of men to jelly and make less brave men a trifle nervous.

"Jelly? Trifle?" slurped Pie-Face, hungrily. Pie-Face was always hungry, even though his stomach had been twisted in knots by the ghoulish scream.

"There's nothing to fear," said the Colonel from under the army blanket he was trying to hide beneath. "W...we've j...just reached the Frightful Forest, th...that's all."

"Sounds nice," Dennis grinned, not about to be frightened by any grisly cry. "Are we going to have a picnic?"

"What? And get eaten to death by wild, hairy horrors?" the Colonel spluttered. "We'll be the picnic if we go out there. I don't fancy being wolfed down by a wolf and I couldn't bear being bitten by a bear."

"And I can't bear your painful puns," Dennis answered, leaping for the door. With the armoured car stopped at the edge of the forest, he had a chance to make a run for it. "Come on, fellas," he yelled and Gnasher, Curly and Pie-Face didn't need to be told twice. (Actually, Pie-Face DID need to be told twice, since he had gone into a nice daydream as soon as the word picnic had been mentioned. He was imagining himself sitting with a hamper full of tasty pies and pastries next to a forest of steak pie trees on top of a pork pie hill, by a gravy stream.) In a flash, they were out of the car and racing into the trees... right into a tree, in Curly's case, with a horrible THUD! Dizzily, he followed his pals deeper into the mist-shrouded forest.

"Only an utter imbecile would risk going into the Frightful Forest," said the Colonel from under his blanket. And he would know, since he was the imbecile that had once tried to spend a camping holiday there. He'd lasted almost an entire minute before being chased out by a ferocious hedgehog. "Best stay in here, laddies. Much safer, by far... Lads? Hello? You've gone awfully quiet."

"That's because they've gone altogether, Colonel, guv," Shambles told him from under his seat.

"Disaster," the Colonel roared. "Losing Dennis twice in one day? I'll have to put myself on report and hand back my medals if we don't get him and his revolting friends back safely. But, out there, in the Frightful Forest, who knows what could happen? What if they run into some vast, grizzly, ravenous creature?"

"From what I've seen of that bunch," Shambles muttered, "I'd say it was just the vast, grizzly, ravenous creature's tough luck!"

As for what actually DID happen when the menaces ran into a vast, grizzly, ravenous creature... well, let's just see, shall we?

"CRASH! CRASH! PUFF! PANT! CRASH!" went the menaces, as they crashed through the trees, racing deeper into the forest.

"CRUNCH! CRUSH! ROAR! GROWL! SPLINTER! CRUNCH!" went the vast, grizzly, ravenous creature that crushed trees in its path like matchsticks.

"SHUSH! LISTEN! SOMETHING'S GOING 'CRUNCH! CRUSH! ROAR! GROWL! SPLINTER! CRUNCH!' OVER THERE," went the menaces.

"SNIFF! SNIFF! MMMMMM!" went the vast, grizzly, ravenous creature, catching scent of menace-flavoured dinner. Then, "CRUNCH! CRUNCH! GRRRROWL! RRRROOOAAARRR!!! CRUNCH! SPLINTER! CRUSH!" it went, as it raced toward the source of the delicious smell (if you can call the smell of three unwashed boys and a flea-ridden dog delicious) and, before they'd even had the chance to go, "CRASH! PUFF! CRASH! PANT! CRASH!" as they ran away, it had gone, "KERRASH!!! SPLINTER!!! ROARRR!!!" and burst out of the trees to block their path.

Then, "GNASH! GNASH! SNARL! GNASHITY-GNASH!" went Gnasher, his teeth going so fast that he was just a blur.

"EEK! SWOON!" went the vast, grizzly, ravenous creature, then, "THUD!" as it fainted to the ground.

"PHEW!" went the menaces, then, "PAT! PAT! PAT!" on Gnasher's head, followed by a, "GNO PROBLEM," from the pleased pooch.

Soon, "KNOCK, KNOCK, KNOCK!" went the door to the armoured car. Funnily enough, "KNOCK, KNOCK, KNOCK!" was the same sound made by the Colonel's and Shamble's knees.

"If that's a vast, grizzly, ravenous creature," called the Colonel, "there's nobody in, so SHOO!"

The door opened and Dennis and pals stuck their grinning faces into the car. "So," gloated the Colonel, "you're back, eh? The Frightful Forest too terrifying for the world's so-called greatest menace, eh?"

"Nope," said Dennis, hopping into his seat. "We just began to think this holiday might turn out to be a lot of fun after all."

"Yeah," Curly laughed. "Can't wait to visit Lake Lethal and Perilous Peak!"

"And the Phantom of 'Orrible Oliver," Pie-Face added. "I can't wait to see him... unless he's an invisible ghost, then I'll just have to listen to his scary moaning! Great!"

The Colonel couldn't believe what he was hearing. After all the trouble they'd caused him! After all the escaping! After he'd nearly confiscated his own medals! After he'd been pelted with fleas (remember those fleas?)! They were looking forward to Fort Fearsome??? That was it! He couldn't hold back any more!

"ITCHY-WITCHY-ITCHY-WOOOOOOOOOOOOOOOOOOOOOOOOO!!!" he yelled!

Chapter Four

G rim Fort Fearsome looked like the kind of castle you would see in a horror film, only Count Dracula would've found it too gloomy to stay in. Thirteen tall and crooked towers and turrets jutted up toward the grey, cloudy skies above. There were great, gaping holes in the steep roofs and dozens of windows were cracked or broken. Bats came wheeling and squeaking from under the eaves, bringing down showers of dust and plaster that made them cough and flap their wings in front of their faces (and then plummet to the ground, since they'd forgotten they needed their wings for flying with). Grumbling workmen struggled to patch up the crumbling walls only to find that, just as one cavernous hole was repaired, another section of wall would cave in on the other side of the fort. The rough, tough looking soldiers all wore ugly frowns on their ugly faces while their growling guard dogs snapped angrily. In fact, the only ones who looked happy to be there were the gargoyles, which leered and grinned from every spire, turret and tower. That was until Dennis and his pals arrived in the great courtyard and looked around gleefully. "This is the best holiday ever," Dennis laughed. "So far, we've had a ride in an armoured car, we've seen big, wild, hairy beasts in the woods, we've done a spot of fishing in Lake Lethal," (Pie-Face slurped appreciatively at the memory of the Piranha Pie he'd

scoffed as the armoured car chugged its way up the side of Perilous Peak.) Dennis was making faces at the grey, gaping gargoyles that gazed grotesquely at the gang. "I bet all that stuff about a ghost haunting the fort is true. It looks like the kind of place a ghost would love."

"Ghosts?" chortled the Colonel. "Don't be ridiculous, Dennis! Everyone knows there's no such things as ghosts, isn't that right, old fella?"

The "old fella" the Colonel was talking to nodded in agreement, until he nodded a bit too sharply and his head fell off and rolled away, leaving his body to stumble headlessly and sightlessly after it. The odd thing about him (apart, obviously, from his head falling off and, let's face it, you don't get much odder than that) was that he was dressed in a long cloak, with a big, frilled collar round his now vacant neck.

The head lay there, blushing frantically, as the body's clutching hands tried to pick it up and lifted it by the nose. "Ow! Ow! Ow!" it moaned in an unearthly voice, then, "Other way round, you useless body," it snarled, as it was placed backwards on the severed neck. With a twist, the head was now facing the right way, though still looking utterly embarrassed. It sighed, loudly, then spotted the group of menaces who were watching in astonishment at all this weird head-juggling behaviour. With another sigh, the head drew its lips back into a ghastly grimace and, with a cry of "WHOOO-HOOOOH!!! Beware! Beware ye the curse of Fort Fearsome!" it vanished like a cloud of steam billowing away into the air. Then it reappeared on top of the body, which had forgotten to vanish with it. "Come on, you! Verily, thou art a rotten old excuse for a body," it groaned. It then spotted the menaces, still staring at this unsuccessful vanishing act! "WHOOO-HOOOH!" it repeated, though less threateningly this time. And it didn't even have time to finish its warning about the curse of Fort Fearsome before the body vanished mistily leaving the head to drop with a "plop" to the ground. "Owyah!" it groaned, before dissolving away into nothingness.

"See what I mean?" the Colonel grinned before he and Shambles set about unpacking all of the crates of medals that the Colonel had insisted on bringing (including the medal he awarded himself for remembering to pack the medals). As he left, he chuckled, "No such things as ghosts. Any idiot knows that."

"I can think of one idiot who doesn't know anything," Dennis whispered to his giggling mates. "Especially if he thinks that that wasn't a ghost we just saw."

"Not a very frightening phantom, was he?" Curly noted.

"Aw, give him a chance," Pie-Face said. "It's broad daylight. I'll bet he's much scarier in the dark. All ghosts are."

"Oh-ooh-oh," a voice groaned from a shadowy doorway. For a minute, Dennis expected to see the bodyless head come rolling out toward them. Instead, the head that emerged was still attached to its body, as heads tend to be. This body was stooped and slouching miserably beneath the head, which continued to groan. Together, the head and body made up a little, old man. A very unhappy little, old man. His hair was as white as snow that had been washed extra-white by a special snow-cleaning-and-whitening-machine and he had massive whiskers (called "mutton-chop whiskers"... though not round Pie-Face, who'd just start drooling at the mention of mutton and chops) which made him look like a fed-up walrus. He was dressed in what had once been a very grand tailcoat and top hat, though that once had obviously been a once upon a long, long time ago. What was left of the coat wouldn't have fed a moth on a diet, while the hat was so battered that the top flapped in the breeze like the lid of a flip-top bin.

The old man looked at Dennis, Curly, Pie-Face and Gnasher. "Oh-ooh-oh," he repeated, even less cheerfully than his first unhappy groan. "Oh-ooh-oh, miserable, wretched, sorrowful life! Oooh, misfortune, disaster, doom and gloom," he continued.

"Don't think much of the holiday rep," Curly said, nudging Dennis.

"Holiday?" the old man echoed. "Oh, for a holiday! Oh,

for an escape from this appalling place."

Dennis was fascinated. "Are you a prisoner here?" he asked, hoping that the old man was some kind of Public Enemy that he could get some tips from.

"Worse," groaned the old man. "Much, much worse! I'm the owner!"

"Wicked!" Dennis grinned, meaning "wicked" in the good way.

"Wicked, indeed," replied the glum man, though he meant "wicked" in the bad way and, just to prove it, he added, "Awful, terrible, dreadful, horrible, grim, nasty and yucky! At least if I was a prisoner, I could look forward to being released. But how can I ever hope to get free of this place if no one will buy it? And it's all because of HIM!"

"Who? Me? I didn't do anything," protested Dennis, Curly and Pie-Face all at once. This was their natural reaction since they were so used to being accused of causing any trouble (usually because they had caused it).

"No," the old bloke said. "I'm talking about HIM! Come with me and I'll explain," and he led them from the courtyard, back through the shadowy doorway and into a massive hallway (all except for Gnasher, who'd caught the eye of a particularly glossy-haired lady guard dog and had gone over to compare fleas). If anything, the hallway was even gloomier than the gloomy courtyard. There were candles burning but even they couldn't brighten up the miserable room. Not that light would've made it any more jolly, what with all the stuffed animal heads that peered despondently from the walls and the rusty suits of armour holding whacking great swords and axes.

The old man, who'd introduced himself as Lord Oliver the Thirteenth (unluckily for him), stopped in front of a large portrait of a man with a long nose and tiny, greedy eyes (despite it being an oil painting, the man was no oil painting). The menaces immediately recognised the face. They also recognised the body. They'd only just seen the two of them appearing and disappearing in the courtyard. "This is my ancestor," Lord Oliver the Thirteenth explained, "Lord Oliver

26

the 'Orrible, also known as The Blaggard Of Beanotown, or The Eerie Earl, or That Rotten, Old Swine, Oliver! He's the reason why I'm so unhappy, great creeping, creepy creep that he is! He's haunting me out of house and home! Other earls get to turn their stately homes and castles into tourist attractions but not me! Oh, no! It's bad enough having the forest and the lake and the mountain. Even with them, I could've made this a profitable hotel for adventure holidays. But it's that grotty ghost that's the real problem! Nobody would pay to spend a night here with him wandering the castle."

Dennis was puzzled. "I'm puzzled," he said, which shows that this writer knows what he's talking about. "We've seen the ghost and he's hardly likely to scare everyone off. I've seen more frightening rice puddings than that."

"Me, too," shuddered Pie-Face, remembering a particularly nasty dream he'd had where a giant rice pudding monster had tried to take a bite out of him in revenge for the bite he'd taken out of it (but, luckily for him, he'd been rescued by his Auntie Gladys, who'd clobbered the pud-beast with a welly full of custard).

The Thirteenth Earl drooped even more than before (and he was already pretty droopy, as it was) and replied, "I know that... unfortunately. At least if he was all ghostly and spooky and terrifying, I could advertise the place as a hotel for haunted holidays, where people would pay to be petrified.

"No, he's not scary. He's just incredibly bad tempered! Even before he had his head chopped off, he was always in a foul mood. He was mean and greedy and always complaining, usually because he didn't think he had enough gold and money, which is one thing that really annoys mean and greedy people. So he kept demanding more and more taxes from the villagers. This was what made him the most unpopular earl in the land, except when he was swimming, when he was..."

"We know," the menaces interrupted, remembering that particularly painful joke from Chapter Two.

"Well," continued Oliver, "It's just so depressing, having

him floating about, groaning and moaning and howling. Holidaymakers don't want to be reduced to tears by grumbling ghouls. Same with people who might buy the place. They just don't want hot and cold running groans. And it's not as if I can afford to do the old place up with a lick of paint and some nice, new windows. Not after the last time I tried to put up some cheerful floral wallpaper and a few window boxes and old 'Orrible tore them all down in one of his strops!"

Much as Dennis agreed with the Phantom's dislike of flowered wallpaper and other soppy, softy decorations like window boxes, he felt sorry for the spook's despondent descendant. "Surely, if he was such a miserly old money-grabber when he was alive, he must've left a fortune for his family."

"Oh, there was a fortune, all right," the earl sighed. "All the legends say that the original Oliver had so much gold and jewels that it took him a month to count them all."

"That's nothing," said Curly. "I've got so many socks it takes me two months to count them!"

"But you've only got seven socks," Dennis told him.

"I know," Curly replied, proudly, "but I've never been good at maths, have I?"

"Can I get back to the plot?" Lord Oliver asked impatiently. "There are only another seven chapters left, y'know! I can? Good!

"But, despite the legendary fortune in gold and gems, no-one knows what 'Orrible Oliver did with them! He never spent them, that's for sure. It would've gone against the rules of The Misers' Union and Antisocial Club. But, since the day he died, not a single gold coin of it has been seen by a living soul! And, if his spirit knows where it is, he's too busy whinging to tell anyone. That's why I had to rent the fort out to the army as a military base, even if it does mean I have to put up with them clumping about in their big, heavy boots and yelling orders all the time. But, the thing is, they're so busy being irritable about all the early mornings and orders and having to stand to attention while that Colonel chap has another award presentation to give himself more medals, that a few more grumbles don't make that much difference."

Just then, that Colonel chap marched up with a long list of duties that the lads would be expected to perform during their stay at Fort Fearsome and there were a lot more than a few more grumbles. So many grumbles that the last the menaces saw of the poor old Thirteenth Earl that morning was the ragged top of his top hat waving forlornly to them as he ran for cover.

Chapter Five

An unhappy Dennis and Gnasher were sitting on a saggy bunk in a draughty tower room several hours later, reading the lengthy list of tasks the Colonel had set out for them (only Gnasher wasn't actually reading it, what with him being a dog and everything). It had actually taken Dennis all that time to read as far as he'd got and he was still only two thirds of the way through the thick wodge of paper.

It was full of fun, holiday-type activities like these;

0530 hours: Wake-Up Call. Time to rise and shine– you horrible layabouts!

0545 hours: On Parade in Courtyard

0600 hours: Breakfast

0605 hours: Washing Up Breakfast Dishes

0700 hours: Cleaning Duty in Courtyard (all cobbles to be swept and individually polished, gargoyle dusting and clearing up any fallen slates or coughing bats.)

0800 hours: Colonel's Medal Collection to be polished

1200 hours: Lunch (to be cooked for the regiment)

1230 hours: Lunch Break

1235 hours: More Washing Up

1245 hours: More Medal Polishing

And on and on it went, through cooking dinner, scrubbing the chains in the dungeon, mixing cement and carrying

Stick your name on the sign using these letters!

ABCDEFGHIJKLMNOPQ
RSTUVWXYZaabbccdd
eeffgghhiijjkkllmmnno
ppqqrrssttuuvvwwxyz

cameron

bricks for the workmen and so on, right up to ironing the regiment's uniforms and polishing their boots before bed at midnight.

"I bet Mum and Dad are having a better holiday than this," Dennis mumbled.

(Meanwhile, Dennis's Mum and Dad, along with the parents of Curly and Pie-Face, were very grateful for Bea's nappy-lifeboat. First of all, they were grateful that Dennis's sister had used clean nappies to build it. Second of all, they were grateful that it had carried them safely away from Hurricane Muriel and the wreckage of their luxury yacht and had brought them bobbing ashore at the island they were currently sitting on, looking out at the wide ocean and hoping to see a passing ship or aeroplane. They were so busy looking out, in fact, that only Bea seemed to have noticed that the massive hill at the centre of the island was belching out smoke and that hot, red runny stuff was beginning to pour out of the top. She was too young to pronounce the words "erupting volcano" but she could certainly say, "Uh-oh! Fings are hottin' up round 'ere!" Wasting no time telling the adults, who would only go and panic, she hung the now soggy nappy-boat over a creeper to dry. She had the feeling that they'd need it again pretty soon.)

Curly and Pie-Face had their own saggy bunks in the same room as Dennis, though room was probably far too grand a name for the cramped space they'd been marched into by a squad of guards. It was more like a broom cupboard with bedding (a suspicion confirmed by the collection of brooms, brushes and buckets that were propped up in one corner).

"So much for a fun week of ghost hunting and playing about in the torture chamber," Curly sighed. "We'll hardly have time to breathe with all these jobs we have to do, let alone have any fun."

"We have to get out of here," Pie-Face wailed. "This is worse than... GULP... school! Let's dig a tunnel."

"What with?" Dennis asked. "Funnily enough, I forgot to pack the shovel I usually go on holiday with."

"Aw! Bad luck," said Pie-Face, who had never heard of sarcasm (and, since you couldn't eat it, probably wouldn't have cared if he had). Then he looked excited and said, "I've got a spoon! We could dig with that!"

"Oh, wow!" Curly mumbled. "A spoon? That'll only take us till... FOREVER!" But then he saw the spoon his mate had packed. It was shiny, silver and about three feet wide. "You really are a greedy gannet," he said, in awe of Pie-Face's eating abilities.

Dennis had spotted a flaw or two in the tunnel scheme. "Flaw number one, we're nearly at the top of a tower, so we'd have to tunnel through seven floors and a dungeon before we could dig our way out. Flaw number two, we would then have to dig our way through a mountain. And flaw number three, all this tunnelling would take months and we're only here for a week, so we'd have to keep coming back to finish digging."

Gnasher nodded (or, in Gnasher-Speak, Gnasher gnodded). He knew (gnew) all there was to know (gnow) about tunnelling, since he was forever burying bones (gnosh) or trying to bury postmen (gnits) around Beanotown. So, he gnew how much chance the menaces had of digging their way through an entire mountain. "Gnone at all! Gnope! Gno chance! Gnot in a million years! Gnever! Gnuts to even try!"

Curly had another plan. "When it gets dark, we can sneak out and..." this was the part he was most proud of, "...instead of waiting till night-time, we can just close our eyes. It always gets dark when I close my eyes." He looked round at his despairing pals before admitting, "Okay. I didn't say it was a very good plan."

Dennis was looking thoughtful. This was an expression that struck terror into the hearts of all grown ups, since, when Dennis was thoughtful, his thoughts were always running to mischief, mayhem, menacing and other troublesome antics beginning with "m" (ooh, just thought of another one... misbehaviour)! "What this situation calls for is something so cunningly sneaky and sneakily cunning that it could out-sneak the cunningest sneak in Sneakdom, though it will still

33

involve darkness and a bit of digging... into the past! Listen..."

And, as Curly, Pie-Face and Gnasher listened to Dennis's whispered idea, someone else outside in the corridor had just stopped listening and was creeping down the stairs. Shambles had been passing when he'd just happened to overhear the lads discussing escape plans. The fact that he'd had to press his ear tightly against the door to "just happen" to overhear them didn't make much difference to him. If those kids escaped, Shambles knew exactly who would be sent to find them in the Frightful Forest and there was no way he wanted to risk his skin. It may have been slightly shabby and wrinkly skin that was a bit loose around his bones but it was the only skin he had and it kept his insides nicely in place.

Running as fast as his crooked Cockney legs would carry him (which wasn't very fast at all, as a snail noticed while it waited impatiently for him to get out of the way) he was soon(ish) outside the door to the Colonel's office. He knocked smartly, "KNOCK! KNOCK! KNOCK!" Then he knocked stupidly, "BRRRING! SPLUNGE! PATOWIE!" just for a lark (though the lark didn't find it funny and flew away).

A voice came from behind the door. "Who goes there? Friend or foe?" it demanded.

Shambles thought for a moment, before answering, "Well, I'm a friend to me budgie, Monty, and to the geezers down at the darts club, Nobby, Bert an' Jocko, an' there's Mrs Murgatroyd, down the chip shop an' I'm foe to me bank manager, the taxman an' the bookie an' that great, steamin' nit, Ernie Prunes..."

A little slot opened in the door and a pair of eyes stared beadily down at him. "Hmm..." said the voice, "Where have I seen your face before?"

"It's always been here, on top of me neck an' just beneath me cap," Shambles told the eyes. "It's me, Colonel. Shambles, your 'umble batman, wot's served with you for forty years, man an' boy, though not in that order."

The eyes didn't look convinced. "What's the password?" they asked, suspiciously.

"I've forgotten," said Shambles, who had forgotten that he hadn't been told the password so he could forget it.

"Then you can't come in," the eyes told him.

"Couldn't you just tell me the password?" Shambles enquired.

"No," he was told.

"Why not?"

"Because I've forgotten it too," said the Colonel, coming out of the office and locking the door. "That means I can't come in either. And just in the middle of one of my major military experiments, too. I was working on inventing a glow-in-the-dark toilet seat for use on night time manoeuvres."

"Sounds like a flash in the pan to me," Shambles joked. "You don't want to get bogged down in work like that, though you'll be flushed with pride if you succeed!"

"This is no time for lavatory humour," the Colonel insisted. "If you don't get on with it, Dennis and his cronies will have escaped before you've had a chance to tell me they're planning to escape!"

"How did you know what I was going to tell you?" Shambles wondered.

"Because I was reading this chapter while I was waiting for you to get down the stairs," the Colonel answered, before rubbing his hands in glee. (Glee was the name of a military handcream the Colonel liked wearing, which promised "Softer skin for sensitive soldiers".) "So, they think they can get past my highly trained troops, eh? Excellent! That's exactly what I'd been hoping they would try!"

"Eh???" gasped Shambles, astonished.

"Eh???" gasped Curly and Pie-Face, astonished.

"Gnehh???" gasped Gnasher, also astonished.

While the Colonel had been astonishing Shambles downstairs, Dennis had been busy revealing his cunningly sneaky plan, much to the astonishment of his pals, who were shocked, stunned and speechless.

"I'm shocked," Curly said.

"I'm stunned," Pie-Face said.

"I'm speechless," Gnasher said, which, since he was a

dog, came as no surprise to anyone (unless YOU know a dog that speaks... Ooh, you do NOT, fibber!)

"It'll be the last thing they expect," Dennis laughed. His pals just giggled nervously and looked at Dennis as if he'd gone off his rocker. This plan could NEVER work! Would it?

"My plan worked, just like I always knew it would!" This was the Colonel speaking now, back downstairs in the courtyard. He was talking to the regiment of strapping big soldiers who were standing to attention in front of him (though few were actually paying any attention, just in case the Colonel started telling them all about his years of military service).

"In all my years of military service," the Colonel announced (giving the ones who actually were paying attention time to stop), "and following my many glorious victories," he continued, pointing to the row of medals pinned to his chest (though the row was so long that Shambles had to point to the remaining sixty or seventy feet of medals which curved round the courtyard on a special piece of scaffolding. The little fellow was glad his guvnor hadn't decided to show off and wear all of them), "I believe I have come up with the military master-plan to beat all others." Pausing only to give himself three hearty cheers and a special commendation, he continued, "For you troops are about to be given the best training possible, ensuring that those little lads we brought in this morning don't break free!"

One lone soldier, who hadn't been able to help hearing what the Colonel had said, gasped, "Those kiddies? We're in the army, sir! We can't waste our time looking after children!"

The Colonel spluttered, "Of course you'll look after children! You're in the infantry, aren't you? And, now that that terrible old joke is out of the way, I feel it only fair to warn you chaps that these are no ordinary children (if they were, there wouldn't be a book about them, would there?), no, by Jove, they're not! They are the trickiest, most badly behaved, despicable, troublesome and terrible children in the known world... and some unknown parts as well.

"Your job, my brave lads, will be to stop them escaping! They'll try anything, I tell you! They might build a replica of the fort out of old toilet roll tubes and cereal packets to fool us! They may glue all their bedsprings together and construct a gigantic pogo stick to bounce to freedom! They could inflate their hot water bottles and float away! Or they might tie all the bed sheets together."

"To make a rope and climb out of the window?" Shambles asked.

"No. To stop us getting a decent nap," the Colonel shuddered. "So, be on your look out, men! I've given them so many dull duties to carry out that they'll crack and try to escape at any minute."

Just then, three small figures and a dog joined the first row of troops in the courtyard. They saluted and stood stiffly to attention. The Colonel wondered if he was going bananas. He stared at these figures in their neatly pressed army uniforms and brightly shining boots, nearly swallowing his own moustache in shock. Was he dreaming? He looked round, half expecting his Auntie Gladys to come marching past in her custard filled wellies.

"Cadet Dennis reporting for duty," said the smartly saluting menace.

Chapter Six

Curly, Pie-Face and Dennis looked every inch like soldiers (though they were rather a lot of inches shorter than the other soldiers) in their uniforms and helmets. Only Gnasher wasn't wearing full uniform. Instead, he just wore a cap, khaki flea collar and dog tags.

The Colonel was agog! He was also amazed, astonished and astounded! He would've been bemused, bewildered, dumbfounded, surprised and staggered, but he'd only got as far as "A" in the dictionary.

"What's all this?" the Colonel choked, suspecting that he was beginning to see things that weren't really there because of the fumes from his moustache wax.

"No time for idle chatter, Colonel, sir," Dennis replied briskly, pointing to his watch. "It's 1200 hours, sir! Time to prepare lunch for the troops, sir. Can't miss lunch, sir! An army marches on its stomachs, sir!"

"Really?" Pie-Face asked. "So why do we have all those boots to polish?"

Dennis silenced him with a friendly tap to the shin, which made Pie-Face wince and wonder what an unfriendly tap to the shin would feel like.

"Which way to the kitchens, sir?" Dennis enquired.

Still surprised (having quickly glanced through the "S" section in his dictionary), the Colonel produced a map of the fort from his pocket (having first produced a map of his pockets to help him find it) and pointed them in the direction of the kitchens.

The lads set off in the direction of the pointing finger. On the way, Gnasher winked at the female guard dog he'd met earlier and she flirtatiously flicked her long blonde tail back at him.

The Colonel watched them go, his bristles bristling with suspicion. He quickly woke two soldiers who were sleeping to attention and told them, "Keep a close watch on those youngsters and see they don't get up to any funny business." The two soldiers followed the menaces, though, judging by the jokes so far, they doubted there'd be any funny business in the entire book.

The kitchens were next to the Officer's Mess, though they were a right mess themselves. Military chefs rushed here and there with trays laden with uncooked cooking. Dennis saluted to a huge guard, saying, "Dennis and company reporting for cooking duties, sir!"

"Cooking?" the guard laughed, sounding tickled. He was tickled but it was just the woollen kilt he was wearing. "You laddies won't be cooking. Come with me," and he led them to a cupboard at the back of the kitchen. "In here," he sniggered and opened the door, revealing a room full of potatoes. Thousands of potatoes, all piled up.

"Wow!" Curly gaped. "A lifetime's supply of spud gun ammo!"

"You laddies are on spud bashin' duty," the guard laughed, evilly.

"Why?" asked Pie-Face. "What've they done to you?"

After the guard had explained that spud bashing didn't actually mean bashing, thumping or generally roughing the spuds up a bit but actually meant peeling them, he handed them each a tiny potato peeler and left them alone with all three thousand potatoes.

The menaces stood in the small room, all eyes on the potatoes (though potatoes already have eyes so it didn't make much difference). "This could take a while," Dennis said, "unless..."

Outside, in the kitchen, the two soldiers sent to guard the gang were prepared for several hours of boredom. What they weren't prepared for was the door opening five minutes later and Dennis popping his head round to announce, "All done!" And, sure enough, when they looked, the soldiers saw three thousand peeled white potatoes.

"We'll have time to get a start on the Colonel's medals," Dennis said, saluting to the speechless soldiers and leading the menaces swiftly out of the kitchen.

"How did they do that?" asked one soldier.

"And where did the peelings go?" asked the other.

They were so busy wondering about it that neither noticed that Gnasher and Pie-Face weren't walking as swiftly as the others and that they had both put on a bit of weight. And it's probably just as well they didn't notice since it might've put them off their chips to know that, between them, Gnasher's and Pie-Face's jaws could work a whole lot faster than even the fastest electric potato peeler in the world.

As for the next task, polishing all of the Colonel's many, many medals, that would be a piece of cake (and a piece of cake would've suited Pie-Face as afters for all those potato peelings) since the Colonel had insisted on polishing them all himself before he let anyone else in to polish them. The lads had to put on sunglasses before they could even enter the room, so bright was the glare from hundreds upon hundreds of shining medals.

The Colonel had been decorated many times (which doesn't mean that he'd been given a fresh coat of paint... except for that one time when he'd gone to a military fancy dress ball as the Berlin Wall) for just about any deed you could imagine (and a few you probably couldn't).

The room the Colonel had chosen to store his awards in had obviously been a family portrait gallery. This was obvious from the sign on the door, which said, "Family Portrait Gallery", as well as all the portraits of the morose

Thirteenth Earl's family. All his ancestors looked as thoroughly depressed as he had. Not that Dennis was bothering with the paintings. He was busy reading the neatly typed little labels the Colonel had placed next to each item in his prized collection of prizes. Among them were:

MEDAL FOR TRAINING BEES TO PATRIOTICALLY BUZZ TO THE TUNE OF "RULE BRITANNIA" DURING WARTIME PLUS M.B.E. (MUSICAL BEE EFFORT).

CATERING MEDAL FOR DELIVERING ICE-LOLLIES TO ARCTIC EXPEDITION TEAM.

MEDAL FOR BRAVERY IN THE FACE OF SUPPER (RATIONS OF CURRIED PRUNES AND RHUBARB).

RUNNING MEDAL.

MEDAL FOR KNITTING WOOLLEN "COSIES" TO FIT OVER NELSON'S COLUMN, BIG BEN, STONEHENGE AND THE ALBERT HALL DURING COLD SNAPS.

MOUNTAINEERING MEDAL FOR SWIMMING UP THE NORTH FACE OF EVEREST.

DIVING MEDAL FOR CLIMBING THE LENGTH OF THE NILE.

LIFESAVING MEDAL FOR GIVING THE KISS OF LIFE TO DROWNING COD.

MEDAL FOR BEST AND BRISTLIEST AND WAXIEST MOUSTACHE (PRESENTED BY THE ROYAL HAIR FORCE).

MEDAL FOR GIVING TRANSFUSIONS TO BLOODHOUNDS.

STIFFEST UPPER LIP MEDAL.

INVENTORS' MEDAL FOR "COLONEL'S PATENTED UPPER LIP STIFFENER" (GUARANTEED TO STIFFEN EVEN THE FLOPPIEST, FLABBIEST OR SAGGIEST OF UPPER LIPS).

MEDAL FOR FINDING THE LOST CITY OF ATLANTIS.

MEDAL FOR LOSING THE FOUND CITY OF ATLANTIS AGAIN (AWARDED BY THE ATLAS MAKERS OF THE WORLD, SINCE THEY DIDN'T FANCY REDRAWING ALL THE MAPS).

MEDAL FOR DAFTEST MEDAL COLLECTION.

Curly, meantime, had gotten bored drawing moustaches on all the ladies' portraits and lipstick on all the men's (he always was an artistic child) and was in the mood for moaning again about all the work they'd been given and the guards outside the door. "I mean, what were our mums and dads thinking about, sending us into slavery while they enjoy a leisurely cruise?"

(At that moment, the lads' mums and dads were cruising at a leisurely 60 miles an hour, blown along by a gale of hot air that was caused by the combined screams of three dads and three mums, which pushed a massive sail made from Pie-Face's rather rotund father's Hawaiian shirt, held up by a mast that was actually Dennis's rather skinny dad. Bea, meanwhile, was calmly fishing, using a nappy pin on a string as she tried to hook one of the "fishy-wishies" she'd spotted following the "Good Ship Nappy". These "fishy-wishies" were the reason for all the screaming, since they had actually turned out to be "sharky-warkies"!)

"I mean," Curly was still complaining, "we ARE menaces, aren't we? We should be busting our way out of this crummy castle, not signing up for Lads' Army, or whatever it is that means we have to obey all these stupid orders to peel medals and polish spuds!"

The more Curly talked, the angrier he sounded, until, "What's going on, Dennis? You're doing as the grown ups say! Have you turned into a softy?"

BIIIIGGG MISTAKE!!! Though what I actually mean to say is: BIIIIGGG MISTAKE!!!

Curly knew he shouldn't have said that. He knew it as soon as the words had passed his lips, which were now trembling in terror (he could've done with the "Colonel's Patented Upper Lip Stiffener" right then).

The room had gone awfully quiet and still. Pie-Face had decided to pretend he was dead to avoid getting involved in what happened next. He lay on the floor with his arms folded across his chest, a hastily constructed gravestone at his head (made out of a chair back with the words, "REST IN PIES" scribbled on it) and his eyes tightly shut.

Because his eyes were shut, Pie-Face didn't actually see what went on between Dennis and Curly. But he did hear it and it sounded like this;

"A SOFTY, EH?" BIFF! THUMP! "OW! OW! OOH!" BLAT!

SPLAT! THWACK! "AARGH! S...SORRY... EEK... D...DENNIS!"
THUNK! POW! "WANNA BUST OUT? HOW ABOUT USING YOUR
HEAD AS A BATTERING RAM?" CRASH! "OOOH! ME POOR
NUT!" THUD! "OUCH!" BANG! "OUCH!" KA-THUNK! "OUCH!"
BOOM! "OUCH!" SQUELCH! "AUNTIE GLADYS...?" TWANG!
"EEK!" CLANG! "URGH!" BIFFTHUDCRUNCHBLAMMO!
"GROOOAAANNN!"

Dennis dusted his hands together and said, "Good job
we're mates. If anybody else had called me a softy I
might've got cross."

"Squid, jam, hexagon, bicycle, trombone, cat-flap,"
replied the dazed Curly, who was either still dazed or
reading the weirdest shopping list ever written. "Cuckoo
clock, fishtail, umbrella, hat-stand," he burbled on.

"Breaking out of here is the first thing they'll expect us to
do," Dennis explained again to his pals (he'd already told
them the plan seven times but they weren't the brightest
lads in Beanotown). "If we do as we're told, they'll be so
suspicious that they'll be watching us closely for tricks of
some kind and that's the real trick, since we'll really be
doing just as ordered. They'll soon get fed up watching us
all the time. That's when we make our move!"

"And escape?" Curly asked, since he was beginning to
come round, though he did add, "Fondue, curling tong,
fruitbat."

Dennis sighed. Sometimes his fellow menaces could be
as thick as school cafeteria custard. "No. Not escape," he
said. "If we escape, we can't help old Oliver the Thirteenth
solve the mystery of the missing miser's money so he can
get rid of these soppy soldiers and buy a less haunted
castle... or one with a better spook, at least.

"Those guards are going to be so worn out guarding us
that we can just wait till night time and do a bit of digging
about into the castle's history. I bet there's a clue to the
ghost's gold somewhere! Maybe it's in the castle library..."

"The l...library?" Curly gasped in horror. "Are you mad?
We can't go in there!"

"Why not?" Dennis asked.

"There'll be..." Curly gulped, "b...books! We might I...learn something!"

"Don't worry. Nothing will get through your thick skull," Dennis said, reassuringly. "Anyway, the clue might be anywhere. Even in one of these rotten old paintings. We might as well start here."

"It's a good plan," admitted Pie-face, who had given up playing dead.

"Verily, 'tis a corker," said the figure lying next to Pie-Face in his pretend grave, only this was somebody who wasn't playing at being dead.

"G...g...ghost!!!" howled Pie-Face when he realised he was looking straight into the eyes of the late Lord Oliver the 'Orrible. He leapt to his feet and found himself still staring into those greedy little eyes, even though 'Orrible Oliver's body was still stretched out on the floor.

"Didst I not warn thee to beware of the curse?" demanded the freakily floating head.

"Yes," Dennis said. "Thou didst... I mean, you did."

"Yet still thou darest meddle, young, spiky haired knave?" snarled the ghostly head as it shot across the room to come face to face with Dennis. "Thou wouldst seek the treasure that has been lost these many centuries? Thou wouldst risk that dread and fearful cursed fate that must befall all who wouldst attempt to discover the Ancient Secret Of Fort Fearsome, thou impudent and foolhardy varlet?"

"Who are you calling Violet?" Dennis growled. "And what's with all the funny words? Didst thou swallow a book of Shakespeare? What are we going to get next, rhyming couplets?" Curly, Pie-Face and Gnasher were all surprised that Dennis knew so much about Shakesperian verse. They were even more surprised that they knew so much about it!

"Why don't you go and rattle some chains in the dungeons, mate?" Dennis jeered. "We don't have time for all your mumbo-jumbo."

"Dost thou not fear ye Phantom of Fort Fearsome?" The ghastly floating head sounded furious as it moved even closer to Dennis.

"Phe-ew!" said Dennis, taking a step backwards. "Only your pongy breath! I suppose toothpaste and breath mints hadn't been invented when you were alive, eh?"

Suddenly the Phantom's eyes were ablaze. Now, this isn't just one of those things writers put into books, like, "He spoke in an icy whisper," or, "She gave him a fiery glare," or even, "Her eyes were twin pools of clear, dazzling blue water, her lips were luscious, red cherries and her hair, her glorious blonde hair, it was a field of gently swaying golden corn" (though the last one only appears in sickeningly soppy romance books... ERM... or so I've been told, since, OBVIOUSLY I don't read that kind of mush! Honest!)

No, the Phantom's eyes REALLY WERE ablaze! Two balls of fire burned beneath his angry brows. And, when he spoke, more flames roared out of his mouth! "Ignore my warning at thine own peril, mortals! Reveal the Ancient Secret Of Fort Fearsome and thou wilt find thy own doom!"

Then, with an almighty ROOOOOAAAAARRRR, the ghostly head spun quickly round the room, blasting out a fiery trail that circled the menaces inside a blazing ring in the centre of the vast gallery. Faster and faster it spun until, with a blinding burst of red light, it vanished into thin air.

"He's getting better at the whole scaring malarkey, isn't he?" said Pie-Face, looking awestruck.

"Old hothead? Not really," yawned Dennis, pointing to the floor, where the head (minus fire) had materialised again and was trying to shift the body, which hadn't moved. When it noticed them all looking, it began to whistle, trying to look innocent while whispering through gritted teeth, "Wilt thou waken up, thou lazy body? Verily, thou hast embarrassed me again." Dennis reckoned he could even hear snoring coming from somewhere inside the body's neck, until it finally stirred, sleepily tried to swat the head like an irritating fly, stretched and then disappeared.

"Maybe looking for the treasure's not such a good idea," Pie-Face mumbled, "What with all the curses and doom and dreadful fates and fire breathing and stuff."

Dennis was appalled. "What? You didn't really believe all

that stuff, did you?" The others nodded (except for Gnasher, who gnodded. His fur had been singed and was still smouldering a bit so he gnew the fire-breathing bit was real enough).

"Come on, guys," Dennis said. "He's just trying to scare us off because he knows we're onto something! He's worried that we just might find his hidden fortune. He wasn't that bothered about us until we started talking about looking for clues. Why else would he suddenly pop up and start getting all hot under the collar... well, hot above the collar about it?"

"Maybe because the writer realised that we're quite far into the book and "there hadn't been much in it to give folk the heebie jeebies. I mean, I've hardly had a heebie yet let alone a good jeebie!" suggested Curly (who'd suddenly become a real Smart Aleck who'd better watch it, otherwise the writer might come up with a nasty surprise or two for him in the next couple of chapters!), who immediately changed his mind and said, "Though Dennis is probably right," (clever boy, Curly) and looked around the gallery. "The ghost didn't appear until you started going on about the paintings."

Dennis sprang into action, grinning in triumph. "I knew there'd be a clue! Get looking, menaces! We have to check all these pictures. Let's split up and do a wall each. Just look out for anything odd in any of the paintings."

With so many portraits and landscapes, Dennis reckoned it could take hours, maybe even days, to examine them all.

Two seconds later, "Found it!" cried Pie-Face.

A minute later, after Curly had explained that, yes, it was odd for a woman to have a long, curling moustache and a pipe but that he'd drawn them on with a crayon, the gang were back to the lengthy task of searching for some clue that might be hidden on one of the dusty old canvases.

A couple of hours and a couple of dozen paintings later and they'd still found nothing, as far as Dennis could tell. The only interesting bit, amongst all these ugly ancestors, was when Curly had said, "What's this a picture of?" and they'd all gathered round to have a look.

"Why would anyone paint rubble?" said Pie-Face, squinting up at the grimy little picture. It was a painting of what looked like a dozen or so lumps of tall stone on a hilltop.

"Looks like a bowling alley for dinosaurs," laughed Dennis, then, "Hey, y'know those suits of armour in the hallway? Wouldn't it be great to use them as bowling skittles?"

"Yeah," Pie-Face grinned, "and we could have a cannonball for a bowling ball." And they were so busy planning the GREAT MENACE-BOWL-A-THON that they hardly noticed the time slipping by until the Colonel and ten guards came marching in, glaring at them suspiciously and checking under the tables for hastily concealed tunnels.

Once he'd reassured himself that the room was a tunnel-free zone and that the menaces were really still there (and not cunningly realistic dummies made out of cushions and papier-mâché), the Colonel got round to the important bit; inspecting his medals. Stopping and peering closely at each one (and beaming with pride at every award), he seemed impressed. "Good job, lads. Couldn't have shined them better meself!"

"That's true," Dennis smirked.

"Not much hope of escape for you lads when you see what you're up against, eh?" the Colonel chuckled, pointing to his medals.

"Escape, sir? Us, sir? We don't want to escape, sir," replied Dennis in his most innocent voice. "But it's 1800 hours, sir. We'd better get on with dinner, sir. No time for escaping when there's potatoes that need peeled, sir." Then three menaces and a dog saluted and marched out to the kitchens.

"I don't like this," the Colonel remarked. "Best have fifty men stationed outside the spud cupboard, sergeant!"

For the rest of that day, the menaces worked smartly and efficiently at every task they were set, making the Colonel so suspicious that, by suppertime, the entire regiment of five hundred soldiers stood watch as the gang made five hundred slices of toast and polished one thousand army boots.

Of course, by this point the soldiers were so bored with the lack of action and so tired trailing after the menaces as they raced around being smart and efficient that they were falling asleep (and didn't even notice the shoe polish on their toast and their freshly buttered boots).

That night, Dennis sat on his bunk, delighted by the way his plan was working out. He could hear the guards outside the menaces' broom cupboard snoring already. "We'll sneak out and investigate," he whispered, "in five minutes, when the whole fort's asleep."

Within three minutes, the whole fort WAS asleep... including Dennis, Curly and Pie-Face. All that good behaviour had worn them out totally.

But, if they had been awake, they might have noticed the strange and mysterious things that took place on that long, dark night. Strange, mysterious and ghostly things!

And it all started when Dennis's pants became possessed!

Chapter Seven

Heavy darkness filled the broom cupboard, where an invisible hand rifled through the discarded clothes at the foot of Dennis's bed. The Phantom moved with the sort of silence that only a ghost can have... though it could've marched through the room with cymbals strapped to its knees, blowing a trumpet and setting off fireworks and still not have been heard over the snores of the three sleeping lads. Honestly, they sounded like a roaring grizzly bear setting off a foghorn while revving up a chainsaw.

"Verily," whispered the Phantom of 'Orrible Oliver, "that snoring is enough to wake the dead! Though the dead are already awake and shall surely foil these children's schemes to find the Ancient Secret I have protected these many centuries!"

A pair of clean underpants seemed to float up out of the pile, while the Phantom muttered, "Forsooth, these are indeed strange garments that modern mortals clothe themselves in, yet they shall prove necessary for my masquerade."

If anyone had been awake in that room, they would have been treated to the sight of a pair of pants seemingly pulling themselves upwards to fit snugly around thin air (though Lord Oliver's greed while he was alive had made him a bit on the heavy side so "fat air" might be a better description).

The eerily mobile underpants then dipped out of sight at the foot of the bed, only to pop back up again, this time accompanied by a red and black jumper, which stretched and pulled itself into place above the pants. The jumper was soon joined by a pair of black shorts, which slid up to hide the haunted pants from sight.

The next items to follow these floating clothes into the air were a pair of socks. Invisible fingers dangled the fuming footwear in front of an invisible nose. There was the sound of a wary "SNIFF", followed rapidly by the sound of a painful "THUD" as the invisible head fainted and rolled off the invisible neck, dropping to the floor, where it lay for a moment, turning a sickly shade of invisible green.

When the head slowly came to, it was relieved to see that the socks were safely contained inside Dennis's shoes, which were now being filled by a pair of invisible feet. A red and black-sleeved arm reached down toward the groggy head and an unseen hand carefully lifted it by the ear and plopped it back into place on its neck.

Dennis's clothes strutted round the room and seemed to chuckle to themselves as they crept out of the door, "Now to ensure that this meddlesome menace is seen to live up to his reputation... and that doltish Colonel's expectations!" Then, with a final, chilling laugh, the unseen occupant of the animated clothing closed the door, leaving the menaces to their dreaming and snoring.

At this time, Gnasher, who was neither dreaming nor snoring and wasn't even in the broom cupboard, was enjoying a romantic, candlelit bowl of dog food with the dog of his dreams. Her name was Gnora, he'd discovered, Gnora Bone, and, when she was off duty from guarding things, she enjoyed long walks in the country, nights in front of the fire, burying things and scratching. She liked her men (her dogs, actually) to be well groomed and Gnasher had made a special effort, glossing his wiry hair back with chicken grease to give him a shiny coat AND make him smell irresistible. He'd even brought her a gift of that exotic perfume, KENNEL No. 5.

Now it was time to say their goodnights. All evening they'd been making puppy dog eyes at one another and barking

51

sweet nothings into each other's ear. Was this the moment?

"Gnight, then," said Gnora, reluctantly. "I had a really gnice evening." She closed her big, brown eyes and leaned closer, her lips puckering.

Quickly, Gnasher checked his breath. It smelled of tripe. Phew! That was okay, then. He leaned closer, his lips nearly on hers.

KERASH!!!

THUD!!! THUNK!!!

CLANG!!! CLATTER!!! CLANG!!!

"Gneh?" said Gnasher and Gnora as they both turned to look for the source of the din (and bringing this sugary and slushy, soppy romantic stuff to an end, you'll be relieved to know). "Gnoisy," Gnasher frowned.

"SSSHHHHH!" hissed Gnora, who had gone all tense and whose fur was bristling up on her back. Her teeth bared in a threatening snarl, she tore off toward the continuing CLANGS and CRASHES, which sounded like they were coming from the great entrance hall to the fort's main tower.

More barking rang out as a pack of guard dogs raced out of their kennels and into the courtyard. The barking was followed by the sound of yawns and groans from all around the fort, as soldiers were aroused from their soldiery slumbers by all the clanging and woofing. Doors banged, footsteps raced, there were yells (and quite a few bumps as half-asleep soldiers collided with each other in the corridors). The whole fort had been wakened by the noise.

Well, very nearly the whole fort. In their cramped broom cupboard, the menaces still snored away, completely unaware of the commotion going on outside. They were all far too busy dreaming of causing a commotion themselves.

In the meantime, Gnora and Gnasher had found the huge door to the hall standing ajar. Inside was a disaster area. Sections of suits of armour were scattered all across the marble floor. It looked like something big and heavy had crashed into them, knocking them flying. Then something big and heavy crashed into Gnasher and sent him flying. He landed, head first, in one of the upturned knights' helmets, which luckily muffled the gnaughty gnashings he exploded with.

The big and heavy thing that had crashed into Gnasher was the Colonel's dog, Champion. You could tell he was the Colonel's dog from the way his whiskers had been waxed so that they stood to attention, from all the medals pinned to his collar and from the way he was dragging a half-sleeping Colonel, who straining to grip the leash, behind him.

Champion began to bark orders to the pack of eager hounds gathering at the scene, while the Colonel barked orders to the mob of less than eager soldiers that had slouched onto the scene.

Champion's orders went something like, "Seal off the area to make sure the culprit doesn't get far! Split into twos and search the building from top to bottom! Off y'go, troops!"

The Colonel's orders were almost identical to Champion's (apart from not needing translated from dog-talk) except that he also ordered a cup of nice hot cocoa and a yummy chocolate biscuit while he set about investigating the mysterious mess in the great hall.

"It's as if a bomb went off," both the Colonel and Champion told the soldiers and guard dogs.

Gnasher, who had finally managed to escape from the helmet (luckily he always carried a spare tin opener in case of sudden encounters with dog food), looked around and spotted the cannon ball that was sitting in the corner. A gnasty suspicion grew as he remembered the talk, earlier, about the GREAT MENACE BOWL-A-THON. But, surely Dennis wouldn't have created all this chaos?

Of course Dennis WOULD have created all this chaos. What Gnasher meant was that he couldn't believe Dennis would create all this chaos without inviting him, his loyal and trusting pet pooch, to join in the fun.

Just as he was thinking this, Gnasher heard a slight snigger from around a dark corner in the hallway. He turned and was just in time to see a creeping figure skulk out of sight into the darkness. He only caught a glimpse of the furtive form but that was enough. He'd recognise that jumper, the one with the red and black stripes, absolutely anywhere.

54

Quickly glancing back, he realised that none of the others who were milling about in amongst the wreckage had spotted the sniggering figure's escape. The military men were pretending to listen (the ones who were still pretending to be awake), as the Colonel issued orders and complained about the yummy chocolate biscuits being neither yummy nor chocolatey enough.

The guard dogs, meantime, were listening in rapt attention while Champion delivered the last of his commands. Even Gnora, Gnasher was annoyed to notice (or gnotice), was gazing at the proud canine commander with respect and awe.

"Now who," the Colonel was wondering, "would want to cause mischievous mayhem with such beastly bad behaviour? Not my brave lads in uniform," he continued, glancing around at the sleepy soldiers. "Not his lordship, either," he guessed, as the tiny earl jumped up and down in fury at the state of his antique armour. "The only other people here are the menaces. Hmmm... It's a mystery, this one." (You might remember that, amongst the Colonel's many medals, there WASN'T one awarded for intelligence.)

While the Colonel ponderously pondered the perplexing puzzle, Gnasher slowly sidled toward the dark corner where he'd spotted the culprit sneaking away. He didn't want the Colonel and his men (and dogs) catching Dennis, even if he was a bit gnarked that he'd been left out of the game.

In the corner was a thick, though slightly moth-eaten, woven tapestry. Gnasher didn't know it was a tapestry and just wondered why somebody had put a slightly moth-eaten carpet on the wall. But it was what was behind the tapestry that was more interesting. A low, arched doorway was carved into the wall, leading into a dark and gloomy passageway.

The stone floor was thick with dust. Obviously nobody had used the passage for many years and it had been forgotten about. At least, nobody had used it until tonight. For there, in the dust, were the unmistakable footprints from a pair of shoes Gnasher knew only too well. "Gnuh, oh!" he muttered.

"What have you found there?" asked Gnora, who had just

caught sight of Gnasher's investigation in the corner and had followed him over.

"Gnothing!" yelped Gnasher, trying to sound innocent while also trying to pull the tapestry back into place and conceal the passageway. He failed at both and succeeded in pulling the tapestry down in a crumpled and dusty heap on top of himself. By the time he'd managed to untangle himself, he was surrounded by dogs and guards, all glaring at him suspiciously.

Gnora sniffed at the footmarks in the doorway, before sniffing disdainfully when she saw Gnasher. She saluted to Champion and reported, "Scent of unwashed socks and sneezing powder, sir. I'd say it AAACHOOO!!! I'd say CHOOO!!! I'd say it was..."

"DENNIS!" thundered the Colonel, who had finally had a brainwave (his brain was so distant, all it could do was wave). "He's behind all this!" Quickly presenting himself with a medal for Swift Thinking, he bellowed, "Follow that menace!"

"Left, right, left, right," went the soldiers, marching into the passageway.

"Left, left, right, right, left, left, right, right," went the guard dogs, marching behind them.

"AAAAAAAAAACHOOOOOOOO!!!" went Gnora, suffering from the effects of Dennis's special secret formula extra strong sneezing powder.

"Oh, gno," went Gnasher, realising just how much trouble he and Dennis were in. He was about to follow when Gnora turned back and snarled at him.

"Gnot so fast!" She sounded angry. "So, that was your plan all along, eh? Keeping me distracted while your human got up to all this mischief? Well, you can forget trying to follow us and getting in our way, you... you..." She was trying to find the worst insult she could think of. "You cat loving friend of a postman!"

Gnasher was too stunned by this to answer. He wanted to say that the whole thing was as much of a surprise to him as it was to everyone else, that he had no idea that Dennis had planned any mischief for that night, that he was (for the first time ever) innocent! But, before he could recover his voice, Gnora was gone, following Champion and his doggie patrol.

He could just hear the sound of a distant sneeze as she went.

He was about to race after her and explain when a hand reached down from behind and scooped him up by his neck fur. "Oh, gnickers! Gnabbed!" he gasped, before turning round to gnash the brave or foolish owner of the hand.

Luckily for the current Lord Oliver, who was neither brave nor foolish, his hand was safely encased in an armoured glove. He had been trying to piece together the scattered and muddled suits of armour when his hand had got stuck. "You're going nowhere, young doggie, my lad," his lordship told Gnasher, who was currently dangling by his teeth from the dented gauntlet. "Since your master made this mess, you can help tidy it up. I hope you're good at jigsaws because that lot's going to need sorting out and put together in the right order."

And that's how Gnasher ended up spending a long night trying to figure out which pair of armoured legs went with which armoured body, while also trying to figure out why Dennis had sneakily snuck behind his back for a spot of menacing. And, if that wasn't bad enough, he also had to put up with Oliver the Thirteenth using him as a brush to shine up the assembled suits of armour.

While poor old Gnasher was hard at work, the Phantom Lord Oliver was also working away at his wicked plan. He could easily hear the soldiers following in his tracks (it's not easy to sneak up on someone when there are dozens of you in size eleven army boots). Everything was going exactly the way he hoped. He just had to make sure he left a trail of destruction they couldn't miss. So, as wicked plans went, it would be a fun night for him.

The Colonel was having fun too. He knew that trouble would have to strike sooner or later when Dennis was about and was quite happy to tell everyone about it. He was just glad it was sooner, since he had begun to think he might have to start leaving itching powder next to the boots that needed polished or pea-shooters next to the vegetable cupboard in the kitchens to break Dennis and his friends out of their eerily helpful and obedient mood.

The passageway they were in split into dozens of smaller,

winding tunnels. They were dark and just a bit on the creepy side but that wasn't going to put the Colonel off. Especially since he wasn't going to be searching them himself and had bravely volunteered his troops to split up and do the searching.

The troops weren't too keen on the idea of splitting up, since they'd all heard the stories of the fort being haunted. None of them wanted to run into (or through) some frightening fiend in the dark. Then the Colonel started telling them the story of the time he once tracked a ruthless villain through a similar set of tunnels and they suddenly decided to split up and search thoroughly. Anyone would rather encounter a horrifyingly gory ghoul than listen to another of the Colonel's incredibly boring stories.

"...and the bounder believed I wouldn't dare follow into his underground maze but, by jingo, he hadn't reckoned on my thirst for justice. And despite the risk of being buried alive in a cave-in, I crawled through the deep, dark, dank and dirty tunnels for hours. Sometimes it was so treacherous that I was almost unable to award myself any medals. Then, finally, I had the fiend in my grasp at last. That bunny rabbit wouldn't be pinching any more carrots from the regimental veggie patch in a hurry..." droned the Colonel to absolutely no-one. His voice tailed off and he blinked around in the gloom. "All gone, eh?" he murmured, before slapping himself on the back and beaming, "Well done, old boy. Your tale of bravery has inspired them." Promising himself another medal (and maybe even a big gold cup) when he got back above ground, he marched to the far end of the passage, where he could see a faint glimmer of light from the tunnel opening.

Suddenly the light was blotted out by a figure that darted past. It was there and gone again in seconds but that was long enough for the Colonel to recognise the black shorts and red and black striped jumper.

Chuckling to himself at the thought of all the medals he could claim for single-handedly capturing Dennis in the act of whatever trouble he was currently in the act of causing, the Colonel rushed toward the light.

He emerged from behind a hinged section of wall in the

family gallery, just in time to see the red and black shape dart out of the great doors, slamming them behind him. The draught from this blew the section of the wall closed behind the Colonel, so that it looked just like any of the other walls in the room, all peeling wallpaper and chipped wood panelling, with a picture of a stuffy looking noblewoman hanging on it. "Impressive moustache, madam," the Colonel noted, before looking round for signs of damage.

There were none, or so it appeared at first glance. The paintings were still on the walls, the doors were still on their hinges and the roof was still on. All very reassuring. The Colonel reckoned he must have caught up with the menace before he could have committed whatever crime he'd planned. Yet another medal to add to the collection there.

"Ah, there you are, my beauties," he crooned and his eyes twinkled as he surveyed the rows of military awards, which twinkled back at him. He smiled proudly as he read some of the little labels that reminded him of his distinguished career.

MEDAL FOR BELCHING THE NATIONAL ANTHEM.

Ah, yes. Such a proud moment.

THE MILITARY MORON OF THE YEAR AWARD, FOR LOOPINESS IN BATTLE.

MANGIEST MOUSTACHE MEDAL.

Eh? Something wasn't right here. The Colonel couldn't remember any of these awards.

THE GOLDEN TWIT PRIZE FOR CLUELESSNESS.

THE EUROVISION PONG CONTEST SMELLIEST SOCKS OF THE YEAR AWARD.

MEDAL FOR THE BIGGEST COLLECTION OF TOTALLY USELESS MEDALS EVER WON BY A COMPLETE LOONY.

Someone had replaced all the labels on his carefully catalogued collection. The Colonel's bellow of rage was loud enough to loosen dozens of roof slates, start a minor avalanche down Perilous Peak and cause a wall that had been rebuilt just that morning to crumble into rubble again.

More amazingly, it was also loud enough to be heard over the menaces' roaring snoring and they were surprised to wake up to the sound of "DENNIS!!!"

Chapter Eight

Early morning saw Dennis and his pals under arrest. This wouldn't have come as any big surprise to the citizens of Beanotown, who always knew that the menaces were destined to end up behind bars. It did come as a big surprise to Dennis and his pals, though. I mean, they'd always known that grown ups were a completely different and utterly bonkers species but to suddenly lock them up when they hadn't done anything? It was just plain potty behaviour.

What was worse than being locked in a dungeon, as far as Dennis was concerned, was that Gnasher, for some strange reason, was in a huff with him. Anytime Dennis tried to speak to him, his (up until now) faithful, furry friend would let out the kind of growl that would frighten a cat out of all nine of its lives. This meant that Dennis couldn't ask him what had gone on while he was asleep, why they were all locked in a miserable cell in the vast, cavernous dungeons beneath the fort and why Gnasher's fur smelled of furniture polish. It also meant that Gnasher wouldn't ask his (up until now) loyal owner why he hadn't invited him to join in all the menacing fun or complain about the way he'd succeeded in splitting him up with the lovely Gnora Bone, who was now spending all her time with Champion. So, with neither of them willing to even look at one another, the chances of them working out that someone else had framed Dennis were looking very slim.

The sun was just coming up and Dennis was going over, for the thirtieth time, what a strange night it had been. First of all, there was that angry cry that had wakened him and his mates up. He knew that he'd been asleep up to that point because he could remember talking to his Auntie Gladys about how she was planning to give up wearing custard filled wellies and was thinking of experimenting with a bowler hat full of treacle. The next thing he knew, the door of their broom cupboard had been thrown open and the Colonel had burst in, ranting and raving about armour and labels and how he would see Dennis pay for this, by jingo, yes! And when Dennis had told him he didn't have a clue what he was talking about, the Colonel had seized Dennis's clothes from their heap on the floor and shook them so that little white slips of paper had fallen out, floating to the floor like snowflakes. One had landed on Dennis's pillow and he read:

MEDAL FOR TEACHING SWIMMING TO NERVOUS FISH.

(What he didn't hear was the quiet chuckle of a satisfied spook who had managed, just as the Colonel was discovering the swap of labels on his precious collection, to slip back and leave the "evidence" to be found. The Phantom had to be careful not to laugh his head off, since his body would probably never find it while it was invisible.)

No matter what Dennis had said, the Colonel had made his mind up. The lads were soon surrounded by guards (well, as soon as the Colonel had remembered to go and let them out of the secret passage, which took a while, since the secret panel was so cunningly disguised, since it wouldn't have been much of a secret otherwise) and had been marched down into the depths of the castle and locked in their cell.

Since then, they'd been trying to think of ways out.

"Couldn't we get somebody to send us a cake?" Pie-Face suggested.

"Yeah!" Curly answered. "With a file in it!"

"No. With cream in it," said a puzzled Pie-Face. "I'm starving and I don't think my mum knows how to cook file-cakes."

"Our mums and dads won't help," Curly muttered. "It was them that sent us here. Bet they're enjoying themselves in the sunshine and not stuck in some dank, dripping, gloomy cavern!"

(In fact, Curly couldn't have been more wrong even if he'd said black was white, rain was dry and school dinners were a tasty treat, for, at that very moment, the lads' parents were stuck in what seemed remarkably like a dank, dripping, gloomy cavern. They'd got themselves stuck there after making for what had seemed remarkably like an island. It had seemed remarkably like an island with no signs of any volcanoes, or anything else for that matter. It was just like a big, round, grey rock sticking up out of the water and that had seemed like a remarkably safe place for them to get away from those annoyingly dangerous sharks that had been following them since the previous night.

Sadly, nothing about the island, the cavern or their remarkably good luck in finding a safe place to land was what it had seemed. For a start, the island had turned out to be a massive whale, which had swallowed the nappy-lifeboat and its crew in one big gulp. And the cavern wasn't a cavern at all and was, as you've probably guessed, the stomach of the great whale. And, if you've ever been inside a whale's stomach, you'll realise that it was neither a remarkably lucky nor remarkably safe place to end up.

So, while the grown ups wailed inside the whale, it was up to Bea to think of a plan. It would be easier with some of Dennis's special secret formula extra strong sneezing powder but she would have to make do with what came to hand, which was the Industrial Sized Tub of Talcum Powder Mum always kept with the nappies. So, with an almighty squeeze that sent a massive white cloud up to fill the air, she braced herself against the side of the boat as the whale began to rumble with a great, "AAAAAHHH-AAAAAH... AAAAAAAAAAAAAAAAAAAAAAAAAAAAAAAAAAHHHHHHH... CHOOOOOOOO!!!"

But did any of the adults have the good manners to thank Bea for helping them make a fast getaway from the

whale's stomach? No! They were too busy screaming things like, "HEEEEELLLP!!! WE'RE FLYING!!!")

None of the other plans the lads had come up with were any use, especially Pie-Face's, which were all plans about how they could get their hands on some grub. Curly had said how useful a Cloak of Invisibility would be but Dennis had pointed out that they were in the wrong book for that and they had settled into a gloomy silence again. It looked like they were helpless and nobody was going to come to their aid. Which just goes to show how wrong they could be!

Dennis spotted it first. It was sitting in the corner, just inside the bars. It hadn't been there a minute ago, he was sure of that! Or in any of the other three hundred and seventy minutes that they had been in the cell. Where had it come from? How had it got there? Could it help them out of this tight spot? ("And what is it?" more impatient readers are probably demanding to know. Was it a saw, to cut through the bars? A stick of dynamite, to blow a hole through the wall into the next cavernous room? A gorilla, to rip the door off? A feather, to tickle their guards until they handed over the key? Actually, no, it wasn't any of these.)

"It's a book," Dennis said, picking it up and turning it over (which he wouldn't have been able to do if it had been a gorilla). It was a very old, very large book, bound in leather and full of strange writing in a language he couldn't even begin to read.

Something nudged his arm but, when Dennis turned around, there was no one near him. He looked up and down and up again but there was nobody to be seen. Luckily he looked down again and saw, written in the dust on the floor, "YOU'RE HOLDING IT UPSIDE DOWN!" Just then, the book flipped round in his hands so that the writing was the right way up. Surprised, Dennis dropped the book. At least, he tried to drop the book, though it refused to hit the floor and remained floating in mid-air in front of him.

"I've heard of light reading but this is just ridiculous," quipped Dennis, as the book bobbed up and down in front of his face. Pages flipped over and he saw that the book

64

was "YE HIDEOUS HISTORY OF FORT FEARSOME" by Dame Clarissa Frogthrottler. More pages turned until the book sat open (well, floated open) at a chapter titled "THE SINISTER STANDING STONES". This is what Dennis read:

In the centuries before Lord Oliver the 'Orrible built his fortress atop Perilous Peak, that mysterious mountain already had a frightening reputation throughout the land, for it was here that the ancient wizards held their dark ceremonies. These ceremonies were held at midnight, which explains why they were so dark, within a circle of standing stones. There were thirteen stones in all, twelve of which formed the circle and which were carved with the astrological signs of the Zodiac (Aries, the ram, Taurus, the bull, Gemini, the twins, Cancer, the crab, Leo, the lion, Virgo, the maiden, Libra, the scales, Scorpio, the scorpion, Sagittarius, the hunter, Capricorn, the goat, Aquarius, the water carrier and Pisces, the fish). The thirteenth stone, the altar, had the symbols of the sun and the moon carved into it. What happened to the stones when the fort was built on the site remains a mystery, though some believe that 'Orrible Oliver was so mean that he used them as part of the foundations rather than buy any more bricks than he had to (his legendary meanness also explains how he managed to accidentally cut his own head off with a sword because he wouldn't waste money on a new razor).

Curly and Pie-Face had gathered round and read with Dennis. Gnasher was still in a huff, besides not being able to read, so he passed the time sharpening his teeth on the bars.

"That sounds like that old picture in the gallery," Curly said. "The one of the bowling alley thing."

"Only, it's not a bowling alley thing," Dennis said. "It's a clue thing. Somehow the stone circle is connected to the missing treasure. That's why old 'Orrible wanted to put us off the trail. He knew we were getting close."

"How do you know it's a clue?" Pie-Face asked.

Dennis pointed to the dusty floor again, where somebody had scrawled "IT'S A CLUE."

"Cor," said Curly. "Floating books and messages in the dust. Why can't whoever's trying to help us just TELL US where to look?"

"Somebody is trying to help but I don't think he can just tell us," Dennis explained, "because he'd need a mouth for that." He was pointing.

What he was pointing at was somebody who had materialised out of the air, gripping the book. That somebody was actually the phantom Lord Oliver's body! It stood in front of them, without the bad tempered head on top of its neck, which certainly improved his appearance.

Even Gnasher took notice of this sudden apparition and greeted it by warmly biting it on the shin. But, since the shin was as ghostly as the rest of the body, his teeth passed through it and snapped painfully together with a painful SNAP!

"We can't trust him," Curly whispered (he didn't know why he was whispering, since the body had no ears), "He was supporting that haunting head that tried to scare us off!"

"Is this a trick?" Dennis glowered at the body, which, despite the lack of ears, obviously had some way of hearing, since it tried to shake its lack of head. Realising this wasn't going to work, it stood, scratching thin air where the top of the head should have been, before coming to a decision. With a strange and magical gesture in the air, it made a long feather appear in one pale hand.

"Is that for tickling the guards till they give us the key?" Pie-Face asked.

It wasn't. It was for dipping into the pot of ink, which appeared, hovering by the phantom elbow, then writing on the long piece of parchment, which sprang into being in the other hand. It wrote,

'I'm on your side. It was my head that had you framed and thrown in here!'

Gnasher looked guiltily at Dennis. Dennis looked curiously

at Gnasher. Then they both shrugged and shook hands (well, shook hand and paw). Then, while the others looked discreetly away, they hugged each other tightly and let out a long howl of joy.

The ghostly writing continued.

You have to find the secret, otherwise you'll be locked away for the rest of the week and I'll be trapped here for a whole lot longer! Like eternity! Having to spend all time with that hateful head bossing me round. It's no fun at all, having that pain in the neck on my neck, let me tell you! I had to wait for it to drop off before I could sneak away.

"We can't find any secret trapped in here. Is there a way out?" Dennis asked.

The body didn't have a chance to answer before a grisly cry rang out from somewhere in the fort above. Shivering slightly, it scrawled:

The head's wakened up and it sounds angry. I'd better get back before it gets suspicious. I'll let it think I was just walking in its sleep.

Then it wrote one last thing and scored a thick line beneath it before rushing out, straight through the wall of the cell. The parchment fluttered into Dennis's hand. He looked at it grimly. This was the key to the whole mystery.

SEEK THE THIRTEENTH STONE!!!

Chapter Nine

Yes, the trail of the Ancient Secret of Fort Fearsome was growing warmer but there was still the slight problem of the cell bars, the heavy wooden door which blocked the dungeon entrance, the grim guards on patrol outside and the fact that none of the menaces knew what had happened to the standing stones or what they might look like if they even did find them. But, at least they knew where to look first (after dealing with bars, doors and guards, obviously).

"We need to get another look at that old painting of the stones," Dennis told them. "At least we'll know what those zodiac symbol thingies look like."

Curly pointed out one small problem in that plan (to add to the three large problems of bars door and guards), which was this, "The painting's in the gallery. So are the Colonel's medals and he's got them under even tighter security than us. We'll never get close enough."

"Hmmmm…" Dennis leaned back against the wall at the back of the cell to ponder their plight. Perhaps if they combined Gnasher's and Pie-Face's chewing powers, they could make it through the bars. They could then hide themselves in one of the empty cells and, when the guards spotted them missing and came in to investigate, they could ambush them, pinch their uniforms and, with Curly on Pie-

Face's shoulders and Gnasher on Dennis's, they could slip into the fort undetected. All Dennis would have to do then was sneak into an office with a telephone, call the Colonel while pretending to be a general who was planning to visit and present him with a medal for tidiest fort or something. This would lure the Colonel away long enough to let the menaces nip in and pinch the painting they needed. It was brilliant!

Of course, that wasn't what happened, since, as soon as Dennis leaned back against the wall, there was a click and a rumble and a secret doorway slid open in the brickwork. Actually, "slid" is probably too gentle a word for it. It began as a sliding motion but, with the fort being so old and rundown, it quickly became a toppling, crumbling tumbling as the wall collapsed. Dennis collapsed with it, into a dark tunnel, which opened up beyond it. It was difficult to tell in the gloom but the tunnel seemed to end with a spiral staircase that led upwards into the fort above them.

"That was a real bit of luck," gasped Curly.

Dennis wasn't impressed. "Nah. I reckon it's just the storywriter trying to get us to the end of the plot before he runs out of pages. I'll bet that, by the end of the next sentence, we've found a secret entrance into the gallery and pinched the painting we need to find those strange standing stones!"

Soon enough, Dennis and his friends were back in the network of tunnels, triumphantly holding the ancient painting of the stone circle.

"What did I tell you?" Dennis grinned, examining the painting by the light of the torch he always carried in his pocket for night-time menacing purposes. "Look," he said, pointing to the strange designs painted onto the stones. "The zodiac signs we need to look for. Come on!" And, with that, they set off into the maze of tunnels within the walls of the fort.

What's that, you say? You want to know how the menaces managed to get past the Colonel's heavy security in the gallery and make off with the painting? Oh, all right. If you insist, I suppose I'd better tell you, then... but I really don't think you're going to believe it!

The Colonel certainly couldn't believe it when Dennis had strolled into the gallery from behind a secret panel in the wall and had started to remove a small, ugly painting of some weird stones. He had stared in stunned disbelief from the high, wooden guard tower he'd had specially built so he could monitor his medals behind the highly secure barbed wire fence he'd thrown around them. Sixty armed guards patrolled the fence, while an enormous spotlight swept around the room, and sirens silently waited to go off if anyone even dared breathe on one of his beloved military awards. He was prepared for anything... except for this.

"Halt," roared the Colonel, as Dennis was caught in the full glow of the spotlight.

"Hello, Colonel," Dennis waved. "I just need to borrow this picture," and he'd continued to lower it from its hook.

The Colonel had been about to order his sixty soldiers to seize this small intruder who thought he could just march in and steal paintings from under their very noses when he heard the noise... A strange noise... A noise that went, "SQUELCH..." Then, again, "SQUELCH... SQUELCH... SQUELCH! SQUELCH! SQUELCH!"

An old woman, wrapped in a headscarf and a shawl, wearing wellies that dripped yellowy custard had just SQUELCHed into the room.

"Auntie Gladys?" spluttered the Colonel.

"Don't worry, dearie," came a high-pitched voice from within the headscarf. "You're just having a strange dream. Go back to sleep now."

"Oh, that's a relief," sighed the Colonel, who curled up on the floor of his guard tower and drifted off to sleep, leaving Dennis and the old lady to run and SQUELCH off into the secret passage and slam the panel behind themselves.

"My feet are still soggy with custard," Curly grumbled, as the lads raced deeper into the labyrinth of passageways.

Pie-Face was also grumbling about the waste of good custard but Dennis had known, as soon as they'd found a secret door into the kitchens and spotted the tins of desserts, that they'd found their way to get past the guards. They'd then found the shawl lining Champion's dog basket and had used a folded flag as a headscarf to complete Curly's "Auntie Gladys".

"Which way now?" Curly asked. The tunnel they'd been racing along had branched out and there were two further tunnels to choose from. Dennis shone his torch into the darkness.

Neither tunnel looked particularly inviting. They were both pitch black and covered in heavy curtains of thick cobwebs. There was a dripping sound from somewhere in the distance and slimy water oozed through the cracks and corners of the huge stones that made up the walls.

"Eeny, meeny, miny, mo," began Curly, "Catch a softy by his toe..."

Dennis darted ahead with a muttered, "What's this?" His torch beam had shone on something strange on the wall of one of the passages. He shone the torch between the strange mark on the wall and the painting he held. "Look at this," he whispered.

Curly, Pie-Face and Gnasher looked at it. It was a strange symbol carved into the tall stone pillar at the tunnel entrance. That same mark appeared on one of the standing stones in the painting. In fact, on closer examination, they realised that the rough stone pillar and the stone in the painting were one and the same.

"That's the zodiac sign!" Dennis beamed.

"What, like the hairy ram," Pie-Face gaped, "or Tortoise the bull, or Pieses, the fish pie?"

"Er... yeah," Dennis replied, rather than go through all the signs again with his dim chum. "Let's see where this passage leads us."

Where it led them, after much trudging through the dark and narrow and winding and chilly passageway, was another fork in the path, leading into three further passages. These appeared to slope downwards again, back beneath the fort. The dripping was louder and the menaces could also make out the sound of scuttling and scurrying as rats ducked out of the way of the sudden light from the torch, while twisted shadows danced on the walls.

Dennis ignored all this and let the torch beam fall on another carved symbol on the pillar supporting the middle passage. "This way," he whispered and led the way into the murky darkness.

"OO-ER!" Mumbled Pie-Face, chewing his fingernails, nervously (though he'd rather have been chewing a steak pie, greedily). He didn't much like the sound of all this scuttling and scurrying and slimy dripping, and the shifting shadows around him didn't help. He also had the horrible feeling that they had been followed by something ever since they'd passed that first strange symbol and the feeling had doubled as they'd entered the passageway where they'd discovered the second sign.

(Pie-Face was right to be nervous, since the lads were, in fact, heading toward that most terrifying point in the story... **THE REALLY QUITE SCARY BIT!!!** This would be the part where all the ghost fans who were getting fed up of the Phantom's less than horrifying antics would get something to sink their teeth into. It would also be the part where any softies would give up in fright and go back to reading about talking teddies and flower arranging and singing pixies. And good riddance to the soppy lot of them!)

The menaces didn't know they were destined to discover such horrors ahead. They were too busy following the route through the labyrinth of passages marked out by the ancient zodiac carvings. At each fork in their path, they would choose the one showing a symbol matching those in the painting. And, as they entered each new passage, the darkness seemed to grow even thicker and darker, the coldness seemed to become chillier and the sounds of other things moving around them seemed to grow louder and closer.

A horrid, gurgling, grumbling roar blasted out, so loud that it shook the cobwebs from the walls and brought chunks of rubble tumbling around them.

"Sorry," said Pie-Face, holding his gurgling, grumbling stomach. "I always get hungry when I'm spooked... or when I'm happy, or excited, or glum, or awake, or..."

Curly interrupted, knowing that a list of times when Pie-Face was hungry would keep them occupied till they were all little old men with long white beards (except for Gnasher, who would be a little old dog with long white fur). And they didn't have time for that, right now!

"The twelfth sign," Dennis whispered and they entered what he guessed would be the final passage in their long journey, the one that would lead directly to their goal... the Thirteenth Stone and, finally, the Ancient Secret of Fort Fearsome and the legendary, lost treasure!

All thoughts of curses and ghosts had fled from Dennis's mind, as he raced along the twisting passage. The torch beam spluttered on and off, the batteries finally wearing down. It didn't matter, though, as there was a flickering glow waiting at the end of the arched passageway.

The glow came from thirteen fiery torches lining the walls of a large, circular chamber, an eerie underground vault, seemingly carved into the rock of the mountain itself. At the centre of the chamber lay a long, flat stone, about the height of a coffee table (though you could bet no one had ever used it to drink coffee or tea off. In fact, nobody had ever come into this secret room for a refreshing cup of anything. It was much too scary a room for relaxing drinkies and a chinwag over a biccie).

This was definitely the thirteenth stone that the menaces had been told to look for. They could all see the symbols of the Sun and the Moon carved on top of it. Unfortunately, they could also see something else on top of it and, what's worse, it could see them, too.

"Verily," snarled the palely glowing head of the Phantom, the original Lord Oliver, which was sitting on top of the ancient altar stone, in the centre, between the Sun and the Moon. "Thou art persistent foes, thou interfering, meddling varlets! Thou shouldst have heeded my warning and remained well away from this dark and deadly spot!"

The head floated upwards and across, toward the menaces. It leered, baring teeth that seemed somehow sharper and longer as they gleamed in the flickering light of the blazing torches. Dennis leered back, sticking out a tongue that seemed somehow louder and raspier in the echoey chamber. "THHHHHRRRRAAAAASP!" he blew, rudely. "You're still not scary, you hopeless headcase!"

"We shall see about that," threatened 'Orrible Oliver, just as his body mistily formed beneath his severely sliced throat. "But first, I shall deal with ye treacherous knave who hast betrayed me and led you to this place." Then, much to Dennis and company's surprise, the Phantom raised his foot and kicked his own backside.

This obviously surprised the ghostly body too, since it jumped and nearly sent the head tumbling to the floor. But the head was prepared for this and gripped the frilled collar between its teeth, holding it in place. It sneered, "Foolish body, whilst I am atop thy neck, I control thy movements." This came out as, "Hoowish goddy, hiist I aa atoff hy neck, I cotrow hy novenents," since it's difficult to talk with a mouthful of frilly lace collar.

The Phantom then set about punching and kicking his disobedient body, while the body tried vainly to shake off the furious head. "Traitor!" it growled. "Dost thou think I don't know what is going on under my nose... even when thou art not actually under my nose at the time?" (and I'm not even going to try writing how that all came out through collar clenching clenched teeth!)

Dennis seized his chance. While the Phantom was occupied with beating itself up, he ran to the huge slab of stone lying in the centre of the room. He'd found the thirteenth stone, just as he'd been instructed. But now what? Apart from the emblems of the Sun and the Moon, which had been engraved into the face of the rock centuries before, it just seemed like a normal enough chunk of stone. He couldn't figure out how this was supposed to lead him to the long lost treasure.

Figuring things out wasn't helped by the distraction of

having a ghost floating about, trying to knock its own block off. Every time the head wobbled loose, the body would try to shove it off, only to have it wobble back and regain its control over the mutinous limbs. Eyes were getting poked and fingers were being bitten.

"I've heard of being your own worst enemy but this is just stupid," Dennis said, abandoning his examination of the big rock and thumping it, annoyed.

That did the trick. With the grating sound of rock scraping against rock, the vast boulder began to slowly tilt upwards. There were other sounds too, the sounds of underground gears and chains shifting, as an unseen mechanism raised the stone altar. On and up it rose, until it towered above Dennis, at least ten feet tall.

The menaces gaped in awe but it wasn't at the colossal stone pillar, which had slid into place in the centre of the chamber. It was at what had been uncovered when the stone had tilted up on its hidden gears.

"It's a door!" Curly gasped.

"A door in the floor!" Pie-Face added.

Dennis and Gnasher had obviously immediately realised that it was a door in the floor, since they were already rushing through it and down the stone staircase revealed there when the stone had moved.

Alarmed, the Phantom stopped struggling with itself and soared forward to block the entrance to whatever secret vault lay below even this hidden chamber. This was just too late to halt Curly and Pie-Face in their pursuit of Dennis and Gnasher. They rushed straight on and straight THROUGH the ghostly figure.

"YEEEUUUCKKK!!!" howled the lads, since it's not a pleasant experience, running through someone.

"YEEEEEEEEEEEEEEEEEEEUUUUUUUUUCCCCCKKKKKKKKKKK!!!" howled the Phantom, since it's an even worse experience when you're the one being run through.

Curly and Pie-Face found Dennis and Gnasher at the bottom of the long and winding staircase, gazing in shock at what they'd found there. It was utterly amazing and totally unbelievable!

(And, just to keep you in suspense for a teensy bit longer, I'm not going to reveal just yet what this amazingly unbelievable and unbelievably amazing discovery was. Instead, our story will shift for a moment, since I just know you can't wait to find out what's up with our heroes' families. When we last met them, they were what was up... up at about three hundred feet above the ocean, having been sneezed through the air by a whale.

At least at that height, they were safe from sharks, volcanoes and more whales. Unfortunately, they weren't at all safe from aeroplanes, and had found themselves snagged on the wing of a passenger flight heading for some faraway land. "I hope it's a faraway land close to home," Dennis's mum said.

Sadly, it was a furtheraway faraway land than that and they'd been dragged on the wing over several thousand miles before coming in to land. Even sadder than that, though, was the fact that when customs in this faraway land discovered that the families had arrived without passports, they'd immediately hooked the lifeboat onto the wing of a plane which was flying back to Britain, which is where they were, thousands of feet in the air, just as Dennis and his gang had made their unbelievable and amazing discovery.)

"Unbelievable!" gasped Curly.

"Amazing!" whispered Pie-Face.

The room they were in was much larger than the chamber above. It was a vast cavern, as large as a cathedral, deep within the mountain itself. From high crags and jagged alcoves, fiery torches flickered. The light from these was reflected back from hundreds upon hundreds of thousands of gleaming surfaces, piled from the floor in teetering towers that reached almost to the roof.

"Gold!" Dennis yelped. "Heaps and heaps of gold coins! The missing treasure! We've done it, lads! We've found the Ancient Secret Of Fort Fearsome!"

"You fools!" screeched the Phantom, swooping down and across the massive vault, soaring wildly between Dennis and the mounds of gold coins. "The treasure is not ye Ancient Secret!"

"Then what is?" Dennis asked, puzzled.

"This is," shrieked the Phantom, as a chilling wind sprang out of nowhere and whipped around the room, making the torchlight splutter and dim. From dark, shadowy corners, dark, shadowy shapes began to creep! Twelve cloaked and hooded figures that seemed to ooze out of the very rock of the mountain.

"The Ancient Secret of Fort Fearsome is that there were already ghosts here when I built it," the Phantom roared. "Ye surprise!"

Chapter Ten

O ur tale now takes a terrifying twist, since a ghost story needs at least a couple of good scares to keep fright fans happy.

CAUTION! NOT SUITABLE FOR SOFTIES OR NERVOUS GROWN UPS!!!

If the idea of reading a chapter filled with grisly ghosts and horrible hauntings is reducing you to a gibbering, shivering Nelly, please read the following SPECIAL SCAREDY-CAT INSTRUCTIONS.

1. Don't panic! It's only a story. Repeat this to yourself at the end of any particularly alarming or collywobbles-inducing sentences.

2. Listen to soothing music while reading. The author particularly recommends "Now That's What I Call Soppy Mush, Volume 42" for its calming effect. So calming, in fact, that you may slip into a coma while listening to it.

3. Replace all the frightening words with non-scary words. Any time the words "Ghost", "Spectre", "Fiend", etc, appear, replace them with the words, "Big, pink, fluffy bunny rabbit."(Specially selected soft alternatives will appear in brackets next to worrying phrases.)

EMERGENCY INSTRUCTION FOR REAL COWARDY CUSTARDS!

If you've followed steps 1, 2, and 3 and still find this chapter too horrifying, READ CAREFULLY;

4. Put this book down and take up knitting!
Still reading?
Good. Just remember, "It's only a story! It's only a story! It's only a story...")

The vast vault echoed with the chilling sound of unearthly laughter, as the shadowy figures crept creepily and clutched their clawed, bony fingers. They didn't seem to be solid forms at all, but vaguely human shaped patches of dark mist. It was only as they began to glide into a circle surrounding Dennis, Curly, Pie-Face and Gnasher, that they formed into real figures. Real figures with eyes the colour of blood blazing from within their hoods! (SPECIAL SOFTY ALTERNATIVE - Those naughty menace boys found themselves in the middle of a lovely tea party that the magical, big, pink, fluffy bunny rabbits were throwing.)

A hideous, rattling sigh hissed out from beneath the hood of one of the creatures and Dennis thought he could see long and crooked teeth moving in the darkness. That was when he realised that the inhuman sigh was the creature's voice. It whispered, "Who dares enter the ancient resting place of the Guardians of the Stones?" ("Would you like some tea?" asked the biggest, pinkest and fluffiest of the bunny rabbits.)

The thing that had spoken moved even closer, its crimson eyes glaring in turn at each of the menaces. This apparition appeared to be the leader, as the other eleven ghosts waited back in the gloom while it inspected the gang. In the murky shadows, these ghosts were no stunners and, when their leader moved into the light, it didn't improve matters.

Its bony, taloned fingers actually were bones, a skeletal hand bleached white over the centuries. Webs, thick, grey and dusty, hung like a veil across the thing's face, though the fiery eyes blazed brightly enough to burn through these. The creature prowled toward the lads, its long robes rustling dryly on the stone floor. There was a pattern on these robes, though it had faded over countless centuries. Still, Dennis thought he recognised a strange symbol in the pattern. Something he had seen only recently. But where?

Sensing that Dennis was the leader of this small group of

intruders, the creature turned to face him and, when it spoke, Dennis caught the smell of age and decay which came in waves on its dead breath. It smelled of old graves and things long dead. Or, "Worse than my sock drawer at home," as Dennis said, holding his nose.

"They are living children," the Phantom Lord Oliver hissed.

"Not for much longer," growled the leading spectre. "None who enter this vault survive!"

"I'm not surprised," said Dennis, "with the pong from your mush, mush!"

There was a hiss of anger from the eleven ghastly figures surrounding the gang. Bone fingers clicked and clawed at the air but the leader held up its own skeletal hand, a signal that held the ghouls back before they could close in and swamp the menaces.

"You are brave, mortal child," whispered the leader. "And also smart, to have found this most secret place! But not smart enough to flee for your own safety. Have no fear, though. That wisdom shall come. You shall learn!"

Dennis glared at the creature. "Oh, no, I won't, mate! You just ask any of my teachers!"

"Yep, we're bottom in all of our classes," said Curly, swelling with pride.

"That's when we bother showing up for our classes," added Pie-Face, "which isn't often. We only go in about twice a week. Less, even, like maybe four times," which just goes to prove that maths classes were amongst the ones he missed most often.

The leader of the creatures roared impatiently and, as his otherworldly voice howled round the entire cavern, he appeared to grow larger and even darker to match it, turning a blacker shade of black. He now loomed, twelve feet tall and swaying from side to side, like a deadly, venomous snake preparing to strike, over the small figures of the lads. His hands had become more claw-like, and these claws snapped viciously at the air above the lads' heads. At the same time, something long and sharp sliced through the back of his robes and curled up behind him, like a massive, spiked tail. (The boss of the bunnies had eaten too many tasty carrots and was now all big and bad tempered.)

"Scorpio," muttered Dennis, finally recognising the ancient symbol in the pattern on the creature's robes, as well as recognising the kind of creature the ghost was slowly transforming into.

"Yessss," the horrible voice replied, and it made a chattering sound like an insect. "We are the Guardians of the Stones. We are the Twelve who watch and wait in this sacred place."

All around the room, the fiendish figures had shifted their shapes until they too matched the Zodiac symbols on their robes. It wasn't a pretty sight, all in all (in fact, I feel a bit queasy just thinking about it). Aries, the ram, sprouted long, curling horns of bone, which burst through the cloth of his hood, while Taurus had swelled into a squat, muscular bull-like creature. Worst of all was Gemini, who howled in agony as another head burst out of its shoulder, a twin to the incredibly ugly skull that was already on top of its neck (disproving the old saying about two heads being better than one).

"Uh-oh!" Curly gulped, eyeing the razor tipped arrow pointing directly at them from Sagittarius's bow. "I don't think our horoscopes are looking too good."

The menaces were totally surrounded by monsters! (The bunnies had put on their fancy dress costumes and didn't they look smart?) This wasn't something Dennis was going to take lying down. "You don't frighten us one little bit," he yelled. This wasn't strictly true, since they did scare Curly and Pie-Face a little bit. Actually, they scared them quite a lot of little bits, which added up into one very big bit. But they weren't going to admit to that... mainly because they were speechless with fear.

"We've already seen what you ghosts can do," Dennis sneered, whirling round to point at the Phantom (who had to duck to stop the pointing finger from knocking his head off). "All you do is creep around and grumble a bit."

"Do not compare us to that foolish spirit," the scorpion monster (Big Boss Bunny) laughed.

"Yes," croaked the Phantom. "Leavest me out of this," and Dennis suddenly realised that the ghostly Lord 'Orrible Oliver was scared of these other supernatural beings. A ghost who was frightened of ghosts?

"He is merely our ssslave," chattered the scorpion beast. "His task is to protect our domain from the prying eyes of mortals and to keep ssecret the magical powers we have possessed since the ancient times, when we were the mightiest wizardsss in these lands!"

The creature snapped a claw inches away from the Phantom's throat. "It is a task he has failed! He isss of no further use to ussss!" ("You're a very silly billy," Boss Bunny scolded the wicked elf, "And we don't want to play with you until you learn some manners.")

The Phantom cried out in terror and sank to his knees on the floor. In fact, he sank a bit too deeply, his ghostly body dipping into the rock up to his waist, but he was too busy pleading to be bothered with how stupid he now looked. "I have served you loyally, masters! I have been your humble slave for many centuries! Who shall guard your resting chamber if I am not here?"

"Those who have outwitted you at every step," the monstrous scorpion growled. "Those who have shown the bravery and cunning to defeat your puny attempts to prevent them finding us. They shall take your place and serve us here throughout the thousands of yearsss to come."

"Who's that, then?" Pie-Face asked.

Dennis had a horrible feeling he knew exactly who the monster meant. "Us," he said, thinking that it sounded like exactly the kind of job he didn't want, being a servant to a bunch of bad tempered ghouls in a smelly old cave. Fighter pilot? Yes! Stunt man? You bet! Demolition Derby driver? Yep! Even working in the Paper Clip Bending Department at his Dad's office sounded like more fun than being a spook's slave. I mean, being able to walk through walls and go see-through and take your own head off so's it could be inside watching a video while you went out and played football, those were the bits that sounded like a laugh. But servant stuff? That just sounded like bringing breakfast in bed for the dead, ironing shrouds and fetching them their copies of "The Sunday Tombs" from the shops.

"You will have all of time to learn to serve," the scorpion creature said, as if reading Dennis's thoughts (or maybe just reading the last paragraph). "Here, you will remain eternally young. Though hundreds of years will pass, you will be the same age forever more."

Curly, whose main worry about growing up was that it would mean being a grown up, liked the sound of that.

"Your spirits will be always as they are now," continued the creature, "once we have ended your lives."

Curly didn't like the sound of that quite as much. "You mean, you're going to...?"

"Kill you, yessss," the creature told him. ("Feed you lots and lots of ice cream and big, wobbly jellies," Big Boss Bunny giggled.)

"Hey," said Pie-Face, "Can I be in the Softy version of this chapter? Only they've got ice cream and big wobbly jellies there!"

"Stick around," said Dennis. An idea was beginning to take shape in his brain. "This is about to get interesting!"

Well, if you call having twelve creeping horrors from beyond the grave (twelve twinkly pixies from the magic forest) suddenly swooping on you and trying to kill you interesting, then interesting is certainly how things got.

The first attack came when the thickly boned tail of the scorpion monster crashed violently downwards, the massively spiked stinger cracking the stone as it struck, inches away from where Dennis was standing. This was the signal the other creatures were waiting for and they advanced on the little gang, their hooked hands grasping and their red eyes glowing evilly (fluffy bunnies, twitching tails, hoppity hop.)

The creature with the Pisces symbol on its robes snapped the tooth filled jaws of its shark-like skull close to Pie-Face, who cried out, "Yuck! I don't fancy a bite! I hate fish-bones!"

"Spare me," yelped the Phantom of Fort Fearsome, who only managed to avoid the claws of a roaring, lion-like creature by swiftly lifting his own head off, letting the claws pass harmlessly through thin air.

This was the chance Dennis had been waiting for. "Over

here," he shouted and the Phantom's body, free of the head's control again, nimbly tossed the still yelping bonce to the waiting menace. Dennis caught it in mid-air then ducked, just as a white claw snapped shut overhead. Tucking the head under his arm to protect it (as well as to muffle its irritating whining) he then rolled to safety outside of the rapidly closing circle of fiends.

"Listen, 'Orrible," Dennis whispered into the ear he dangled the head by, "and do what I tell you, if you want to get out of this in one piece!" He looked across at the headless body, which was dodging monsters here and there. "Okay, if you want to get out of here in two pieces, do as I say, okay?"

"Anything," promised the pathetically sobbing head.

"Right. First of all, you've got to stop haunting this castle," Dennis ordered.

The head managed to look even more miserable and said, "I cannot!"

"Here, monster, monster," Dennis called, wafting the head out like a tasty snack.

"I would! I would, I swear," pleaded the head, "but I cannot leave this place! My bad deeds whilst alive have trapped me here forever. My greed has made this castle my prison and I cannot pass on without making amends for my crimes!"

Dennis thought hard for a moment (which wasn't all that easy to do, since he was being kept on his toes, trying to avoid rampaging beasties). Finally, he had an answer. "If it's your greed for gold that's got you stuck here, you could unstick yourself by giving up your gold! Your descendant, the old bloke that owns this place, could do with the money. That could be your good deed."

The Phantom's head gasped in horror at this idea. Gold had been the love of his life, even when he didn't have any (life, that is. He had plenty of gold). Give it all up? The idea struck him as appalling. Mind you, Dennis's next idea struck him as even worse.

"Now to save all our necks, " Dennis muttered grimly (ignoring the fact that Lord Oliver's neck was long past saving). He called out to Gnasher, Pie-Face and Curly, "Fellas! The game's on! Time for the GREAT MENACE BOWL-A-THON... for real, this time!"

Dennis slowly drew his arm back, tightly gripping the phantom by the ear. "What art thou going to do?" it squeaked.

Surprised that the Phantom hadn't figured it out yet, Dennis just said, "Use your head," before sending that same howling head trundling at great speed, straight toward the skeletal legs of the nearest monster.

"STEEEEERIKE!" yelled the menaces, as the head collided with the creature and the creature immediately stopped being a creature and burst apart into a sack of bones. A sack of very startled bones, at that.

"My turn," yelled Pie-Face, and he scooped up the stunned head just as it rolled feebly toward him. He didn't even give it time to regain enough of its senses to protest, before delivering an over-arm bowl. This sent the shark-headed creature staggering backwards into a goat-horned monster and both collapsed into a jumbled heap of very mixed up skeletal bits and pieces.

"SSSSSSSTOP THISSSSSS!" shrieked the scorpion monster, scuttling forward on the six, white-boned legs that shredded through its robe. "We are the Guardiansssss of the Sssssstonesss! We protect the magic of the ssstone circle! Without ussss, the magic will die!" ("Ooh, you rotten rotters!" grumbled the cross bunny, stamping its foot.)

"Ah, shut up, you big bug-eyed bug," yelled Dennis, just as he fired off a cannon-ball shot with the, by now, happily unconscious head.

What none of the menaces realised was that, above them, in the secret tunnels beneath the fort, strange rumblings were building. One by one, as the creatures in the vault went to pieces, the ancient stones that had once formed the standing circle were shaking themselves apart. They were cracking and crumbling and flaking into dust, now that the magical forces that had kept them strong throughout century after century were being defeated. And, if the menaces had realised this was happening, they might not have thought too much about it. Which would've been silly, since these stones were being used as pillars to support the roofs of the tunnels, which also happened to be supporting the entire fort above them!

Of course, not knowing that disaster was poised above their heads, the lads continued their dreadful attack on the now defenceless monsters. They bowled! They threw! The Phantom's body even used the head like a football, firing off shot after shot. (The fact that he continued to do this after all the monsters had been reduced to dusty heaps just goes to show how much he and his head didn't get on.)

Finally, the body stopped giving the head a hard time and went for a lap of honour round the cavern. The lads wiped their brows and patted each other on the backs. The monstrous threat was no more.

Or was it?

"How do we know they'll stay beaten?" Curly asked. "What if they can just supernaturally pull themselves back together?"

There was a very long, very loud and very satisfied, "BUUUUUURRPP!!!" from behind them. (Much louder than that, honestly!)

BUUURRPP!!

(That's more like it!)

"That's how we know," Dennis laughed, pointing at a hugely bloated Gnasher, who sat amidst a pile of empty old robes. Of the bones, there was no sign.

Up above, there was a very long, very loud, very ominous "RRRUMBLE!!!" though Dennis just imagined it was Gnasher's stomach groaning. The soldiers in Fort Fearsome didn't make the same mistake. Once the old building started shaking, they started running for the exit. They would only have a few minutes to wait before they saw what it was they were running from.

But, just before that, beneath their very army-booted feet, Dennis had wakened the head up (just as it had begun to dream of ye Auntye Gladys and her custarde filled bootes) and reminded it of their deal. The head tried for a minute or two to pretend it was suffering from amnesia, "from ye blowes to my head," but Dennis had threatened it with being the ball in a basketball marathon and it quickly gave in. "Verily well," it sulked. "The living lord of Fort Fearsome shall have ye gold!"

So, just before he finally vanished from Fort Fearsome for good (and just after he'd finished arguing with his body, which absolutely refused to go anywhere with him from then on), the phantom head muttered a magic word that caused the gold to twinkle and sparkle out of existence in the vault and reappear in the hallway of the castle. This was a big mistake, since all that extra weight on the unsupported floor brought the whole castle crashing down into the tunnels below!

Chapter Eleven

Keeping as stiff an upper lip as possible, the Colonel led his troops into the trucks that waited to take them away from Fort Fearsome, which was no longer an army base. In fact, it was no longer much of anything, other than rubble.

Lord Oliver the Thirteenth had been furious at the destruction of his ancestral home for a full twenty-two and a half seconds. Then it had started raining gold coins, which had cheered him up considerably. In fact, he even managed to smile for the first time in sixty years, though this might have been because he was thoroughly dazed by all those heavy gold coins dropping on his head.

After he'd regained consciousness, his lordship had listened attentively while Dennis and his pals had told him all about their awesome adventure in the vault of horrors within Perilous Peak. How had they survived the castle's collapse into the tunnels (apart from the fact that Dennis was the star of the book, so it wasn't very likely that he'd be killed off in the last couple of chapters)?

So Dennis had told him of the moment when the roof of the cavern had cracked and split and jagged lumps of rock had fallen all around them. Luckily for them, rocks and rubble weren't the only things falling. Among the more useful items was one of the Colonel's usually useless inventions, a four-seater cannon, which he'd designed to fire men into battle without the need for aeroplanes. It was a proud moment for the Colonel, when he heard how his device had rocketed Dennis and company to safety through the collapsing castle floor. It was a much less proud moment for him, though, when he heard how, two seconds after the menaces had shot out of the barrel, the whole thing had blown itself up, causing the colossal explosion which had succeeded in blowing apart the few bits of the fort which had managed to survive the cave-in.

Lord Oliver was far too busy scooping up gold to worry about little things like explosions. And, when he heard that his phantom ancestor was finally gone for good, the elderly earl had grinned so widely that his false teeth had dropped out and rolled down the mountain into Lake Lethal (where they surprised a large crocodile who was used to doing the biting and not being bitten).

He'd beamed, gummily, "I'm abfowudewy dewighded, wads," (which is what "I'm absolutely delighted, lads," sounds like when your false teeth are at the bottom of a lake clamped into the bottom of a crocodile.) "Now I cam build a bwam mew caffle, inftead of a cwumbwing wuin. Fatewide tewwywifion in ewewy woom, a nife wefepfion defk and a fwimming pool fow all the gueftf. Fawewell Fowt Feawfome. Fwom now on, it'w be Hotew Feawfome!" (or, "Now I can build a brand new castle, instead of a crumbling ruin. Satellite television in every room, a nice reception desk and a swimming pool for all the guests. Farewell Fort Fearsome. From now on, it'll be Hotel Fearsome!")

The Colonel, realising that reserving five star hotel rooms for five hundred soldiers was going to be a bit pricey, had decided there and then that it was time to retreat before the bill arrived. He was just going to have to turn his house into a temporary fort for the time being. Lucky he had a spare room. In fact, since his beloved medal collection had been blown away with the rest of the fort (much to the delight of Shambles, who hadn't fancied packing each and every one into little, cotton wool filled parcels for the journey), he had rather a lot of spare room. (As to what had happened to the medals after the explosion had blasted them into the skies, well, they had to come down somewhere, didn't they? And, at that very moment, large groups of big, wild, furry creatures were going about the Frightful Forest showing off their special medals for "bigness", "wildness" and "furryness".)

Gnasher had tried to get close enough to Gnora to bark his goodbyes but was rather annoyed to find her sharing her dog bowl with that stuck up British Bulldog, Champion. The annoyance didn't last long though, since another, even more annoyed looking dog showed up and demanded to know just what was going on. Things weren't looking too good for old Champ, who had no idea that Gnora already had a boyfriend, let alone the fact that he was a Boxer.

So, Dennis, Gnasher, Curly and Pie-Face waved goodbye to a merrily dancing Lord Oliver, who was busily flashing a dazzling smile at anyone and anything that cared to look. The smile was dazzling because he'd immediately had his old, ill-fitting false teeth replaced by a set of solid gold dentures. These weighed so much that he'd had to hire a new butler to close his mouth for him. He didn't seem to mind that this new butler had no head. That meant one less mouth to feed. Dennis grinned and the happily headless body of the former Phantom of Fort Fearsome gave a cheery thumbs up to the departing menaces and the trucks began the long drive down the mountainside, across the bridge, through the forest and on towards Beanotown.

(At that moment, several thousand feet above them, a jumbo jet was also heading toward Beanotown. Inside, a hundred or so happy holidaymakers sipped ice cold drinks or looked out of the windows at the fluffy clouds they were passing over. Outside, half a dozen or so not-at-all happy holidaymakers chipped ice from their noses and gazed in terror at the fluffy clouds they were about to drop through at any moment.

With a final RRRRRRRRRRRRIIIIIIPPPP, the frayed edge of the nappy-lifeboat/airship tore free of the jet wing and, with a final SSSSSSCCCRRRRREEEEAM, three sets of parents began to plummet downwards. Bea also let out a scream, though her scream sounded suspiciously like, "GERONIMO!" And, with a swift flick of a safety pin, the nappy-craft flipped inside out and transformed itself into a nappy parachute. Seven pairs of hands grabbed hold of the nappy-chute and the menaces' families drifted toward home.)

The last of the trucks pulled up outside Dennis's house. Well, actually, it didn't really pull up, it more sort of slowed down a little bit as the menaces were ejected by a squad of great big muscle-bound soldiers. These muscle-bound soldiers had been reduced to quivering piles of jelly by a little game Dennis had invented to pass the time on their long journey into town. (The game is too complicated to describe here, but it was a little bit like leapfrog, a little bit like blind-man's-buff and more than a little bit like boxing.) The second the gang's rear ends hit the pavement, the truck revved up to one hundred and twenty miles an hour and sped off, only to be chased and caught by the Beanotown police force. This was pretty good going, since the Beanotown police force was Sergeant Slipper and he was on a bike at the time.

"Our folks are away till the end of the week," said Dennis, picking himself up off the ground and heading toward his deserted, adult-free house. "That leaves us with a few good days' worth of unsupervised menacing time!" He rubbed his hands with glee. though not the colonel's handcream, Menaces DO NOT MOISTURISE!

Just then, there was a loud crash from somewhere inside the house, as if something large had dropped through the roof, or several large somethings, as it turned out.

"Hello, Dennis," said a familiar voice, as Dennis rushed into the sitting room. It was a good job that the voice was familiar, since clouds of dust and plaster filled the room, making it impossible to see who had spoken. What Dennis could see, though, was his parents' bedroom through the huge hole in the ceiling. Beyond that, he could see the attic through the hole in the bedroom ceiling and, beyond that, the sky, through the other huge hole in the roof.

What he couldn't see was the tangle of parents and nappies that had crash-landed on the sofa. "We... er," coughed Dad, through the plaster dust, "we just dropped in to see how you were doing."

"Great. Fantastic. Superb," said Dennis, not meaning a word of it. "How was the trip?" he added, not caring a jot about it.

"Dead borin'," scowled Bea, who jumped down from the heap of dazed grown ups and wandered away to play with her toys.

"Boring?" goggled Dad. After a hurricane, a volcano, narrowly avoiding being eaten by sharks, narrowly succeeding in being eaten by a whale and being dragged this way and that on the wing of an aeroplane, she thought it was boring? Just wait till Dennis heard all about their misadventures, then he'd... Hang on, though, Dad suddenly thought. "Yes, pretty boring," he agreed. After all, if Dennis knew what they'd been through, he'd just want to come with them next year and, if they could manage a disaster like that on their own, imagine how much worse it would be with Dennis on board!

Dennis didn't particularly want to hear about some stupid grown up holiday, though. He was too busy thinking about all the scrapes he and his mates had gotten into at Fort Fearsome. He didn't know quite how he was going to top a holiday like that one, with ghosts and curses and magic and all. But, never one to give up hope, he was soon in his room with an atlas, checking out how far away Transylvania was from Beanotown.

That was when he heard an odd KNOCK, KNOCK! What was odd about it was that it was on the window and what was odd about that was that his room (and his window) was upstairs.

"Excuse me, earthling," said the green, multi-tentacled alien that was leaning out of the rolled down driver's window of the sleek spaceship hovering outside Dennis's house. "Could you give me directions to the planet Zzzasquazzzon? Only I seem to have got myself a bit lost in this galaxy! Must've taken a wrong turning around Betelguese."

Dennis looked with wide eyes at the alien being. The alien being looked with seven of its eyes at Dennis (the other fourteen were busily trying to make some sort of sense of a fold-out map of the universe). Dennis looked at Gnasher. Both Dennis and Gnasher looked round for any sign of Auntie Gladys

or even just tell-tale custardy boot marks. There were none, so it obviously wasn't a dream.

"Tell you what," said Dennis, winking to his canine companion, "I'm no good at giving directions. We'd better just show you, instead."

And so, after stopping off at Pie-Face's and Curly's houses, three menaces and a dog were soon zooming through hyperspace at a billion light years per second, heading for a far- off galaxy. Little could they suspect that a vast invasion force of Cyberslugoid Laser Cruisers were waiting beyond the third moon of Zzzasquazzzon to launch an attack and that they would be called upon to save the entire universe by... (OOPS! We seem to have run out of book here, so that'll just have to be another story for another day, eh?)

The End